VIOLET RED

Book One:
First Comes Obsession

Derek L. Davis

ISBN: 9798841674719

Editing by Derek L. Davis
Book cover image by Sameera Madushan
Book design by Derek L. Davis

Printed and bound in the United States of America

Published by Derek L. Davis
2019 4th Avenue East
West Fargo, ND 58078

www.facebook.com/writerderekldavis

CONTENT WARNING:

Please be advised this book is not for everyone. The following elements are a part of the story:

- Child abuse
- Explicit death scenes
- Homophobia
- Racism

The statements and opinions of the fictional characters in this book are not necessarily those held by the author. For any questions concerning anything in the book, please contact the author **via private message** on his social media pages. If a reasonable number of messages are received, the author may do a live stream with those who desire to be involved.

Also Written by Derek L. Davis:

Evil Has A Target
Their Eyes Were Black
Time Stands Still: A Collection of Stories Old and New

Available on Amazon

To Jill, whose work with antiques and estate sales was partially responsible for the creation of this story!

-1-

It's an amusing thing to witness when a person complains in the summer just how unbearably hot it can get and follow up their whining by praying for a dull, cold winter. And then, as soon as the cold months of the year arrive expectedly on their doorstep, complain about how unbearably cold it gets. It reveals something about the human nature - how nothing can completely satisfy a person. A temperature drop, and suddenly you need the comfort of a warm blanket. A rise in temperature will spark the undying need of a cold soda or a cold coffee from your favorite coffee shop.

It isn't just the change of temperature which speaks volumes of humanity, but it is how people can change over time. They may have an even temper, a contentedness that seems to stay for several seasons, but something changes so drastically it takes you by surprise. This is the basic way of people, though. Nothing stays the same, or at least it shouldn't.

The people living in Grand Rapids are the same as the folks who live in other neighborhoods. They walk the streets, silently complaining about the change in the temperature. Older gentlemen gripe about their knees not being the way they should and associate the body aches with the God-awful chill. In the summer, teenagers walk the family dog and sweat profusely, silently muttering to themselves how being in this heat is torture for them, never mind the poor Dachshund being forced to touch the hot pavement.

Terri Connors is a people-watcher. She loves watching the people in her neighborhood interact with one another as they went about their lives, but today was different. There was hardly anybody outside, save for a couple children leaving the warmth of their home.

She looked outside of the window on a cold, December morning and yawned. Half-awake and nursing a warm cup of coffee in her hand, she smiled as she saw the kids from across the street beginning to throw snowballs at each other, laughing and screaming, just like typical elementary-school children. One of the kids—she thought it was Briton—stumbled and fell right in the snow. The other kid—Dexter, was it? She couldn't remember his name—threw another snowball at his brother. She enjoyed watching the two brothers playing outside and had tried (as best as she could) numerous times to get her daughter, Amanda, to join them. But she wasn't interested in throwing snowballs or making snow angels. No, Amanda was content with staying indoors and playing Day-Care with her dolls and stuffed animals.

Amanda took after her, that was for sure. She had short, wavy brunette hair and her laugh was eerily similar to Terri's. Like mother, like daughter. Terri sat down her coffee cup at the table in the kitchen, stomach grumbling. In just a few hours, Terri would be heading to work, stocking shelves in the antique store she owned and taking care of customers. She loved her job. She couldn't think of anything else she would rather be doing.

The arms of her partner embraced her from behind, causing Terri to jump slightly. Delana Burton laughed softly and kissed her partner on the back of her neck, like she normally did on a Saturday morning. Terri returned the laugh and turned around to face the most beautiful woman in the world.

"Did I scare you, sweetheart?" teased Delana, smiling devilishly.

"Oh, not at all. I was planning on jumping out of my skin at ten in the morning. Gets me ready for the day."

Delana grabbed Terri gently on both sides of her face and kissed her on the lips. "Planning on going into the store in an hour?"

"Yeah, there are a couple things I want to do for the start of the season. Do some decorating, make up a display, that sort of thing. I know I don't normally—"

"Work on Saturdays?"

"Yeah. I want to spend more time with Carla, get to know her. Make sure she's comfortable taking care of things."

"I'm sure she'll be fine," Delana reassured her. Sometimes Terri could worry too much about things. "I just hope you aren't working too hard."

"Never," Terri smiled. "But she is a new hire and I want her to be as comfortable as possible."

"Amanda still in her room?"

"Holed up in her room, playing with her dolls."

"I think I'll take her along with me," Terri mused out loud. She only had a weekend to spend with her daughter, until she had to go back home to her ex-husband, Jeff Toms. Every moment she could spend with Amanda was precious to her.

"Not a bad idea," replied Delana. "Amanda isn't too interested in baking cookies or drinking tea with me when you're working."

"She's not that kind of kid, I suppose."

"And neither are you that kind of adult," Delana teased. As much as Delana tried to get Amanda to bond with her, she didn't seem all too interested in the things Delana thought she would be interested in doing. It didn't really bother her, but sometimes she wondered about the girl.

"I think we'll head out in about an hour," Terri said, looking at the clock on the mantle a few feet away from her.

"Give us some time and eat, watch the morning news."

"I'll cook some bacon and eggs for us, then," Delana said, heading into the kitchen. As she left the living room to prepare breakfast, Amanda's door opened. Yawning, she went to the living room and gave her mom a big hug.

"Morning, sunshine. How are the animals this morning?"

"Tired. And hungry," Amanda replied, yawning as she spoke.

"You wanna come to the antique store with me after we eat some breakfast?"

"Are you getting any toys today?"

Terri grinned. "You never know! We just might get another member of the Stuffingtons if we're lucky!"

Stuffingtons was the family name of the animals Amanda kept in her room. When Amanda announced the family name of her stuffed animal collections, Terri couldn't help but laugh a little. It was a cute name, and she loved it just as much as her daughter did. It was a cute, logical name for a stuffed animal family.

"I hope there's a stuffed dog!" exclaimed Amanda.

Terri scrunched her face and said in a sing-song voice, "But what if it's a bear?"

"Mom!" Amanda whined, "I've got, like, hundreds of stuffed bears. I want a stuffed dog!"

"Amanda," Terri said sternly. "No whining. And besides, you love stuffed bears. I thought they were your favorite?"

"Yeah," Amanda said, looking sad. "But I need a dog."

"We'll see, okay?" Terri smiled. "You never know what you will find at the store, and I bet you will find something so beautiful you'll forget all about the stuffed dog."

"It's gonna be a stuffed dog, I just know it," said the little girl.

"Oh, you do?"

"I'm psycho. I just know I will find a stuffed dog!"

"You mean you're psychic. Psycho is something completely different. You don't wanna be psycho."

"OK. I'm psychocic."

Terri couldn't help but laugh. Her daughter always made her laugh.

"Okay. If you find a stuffed dog, it's yours. But not 'til Christmas, okay?"

"Yes, Mommy," Amanda said, excited to explore the new things she knew she would find at the antique shop.

NOT MUCH LATER, Terri took her beat-up green sedan and her daughter to TerriRific Antiques. As the sedan pulled its way into the strip mall parking lot, the voice of her ex-husband invaded her mind – "What a dumb name for a store. You couldn't think of anything more creative?"

Without thinking, Terri found herself shaking her head as she opened the car door, letting herself and Amanda out of the cold car. Shivering, Amanda slowly walked over to the door to the antique shop.

"Amanda, please stick close to me!" Terri called out. The sound of her mother's voice caused her to turn around and she slipped.

"Jesus," Terri whispered as she carefully made her way to her fallen daughter. "Are you hurt?"

"No," replied Amanda. "I didn't fall that hard."

Unconvinced, and acting like the worrywart she was, she took Amanda's hand and slowly walked to the front door. As soon as they entered the shop, Terri lifted Amanda up to the counter and removed her winter clothes, checking Amanda's arms and legs for anything worrisome. The local news was playing in the background – something about a missing woman and her daughter was mentioned – as she continued her search for anything serious.

Nothing.

But that doesn't mean she won't bruise, Terri reminded herself.

The sound of a box falling caught Terri's attention. She

turned toward the back, entering the back room. Carla was there, removing several items from a rather large box and writing down the incoming items she received only two minutes ago.

Carla turned her head slightly, regarding her boss. "Sorry, Terri. The guy that came in a moment ago wasn't too careful with stacking the boxes."

"It's all right," Terri said, frowning. "I didn't hear glass breaking. It happens to me, more often than I'd like to admit."

Carla laughed. "Have you ever, you know…" she had a hard time choking out the next word, making Terri smile amusedly. "Um, broken anything?"

"It was the second week in, and this woman brought in a couple flower vases," Terri began. "I knocked them over and they smashed into pieces."

"Oh no!" exclaimed Carla. "I hope they weren't extremely valuable!"

"Not sure about that. Even the woman said they were ugly, so it wasn't that big of a loss."

"She didn't bitch?"

"She laughed. Called it poetic justice. They were her grandmother's vases, and she was not a nice person."

"But still…" Carla's voice trailed off at the sound of someone coming into the store.

"I got it. Keep doing what you're doing," Terri called out as she took notice of the customer. The black woman held a medium-sized box in her arms, setting it down on the countertop. She looked maybe a few years older than Terri. The woman wore pink lipstick that didn't match the harsh, judgmental look in her eyes. She seemed like she just wanted to donate and run out of the store.

"Welcome to TerriRific Anti—"

"Yeah, so how exactly does this work?" The woman responded, her amber eyes burning into Terri's soul.

"Well, you can just leave the box here and—"

"Do I get store credit for anything? A discount on the small inventory you have on display?" She folded her arms.

"Well, no." Terri reached from under her and pulled out a form and a pen from the cup next to the register. "If you could fill this form out and—"

"Look, miss, I don't have a lot of time. I got things I need to do in five minutes, and I can't be bothered too long," the woman snapped. "Can't I just leave this here and go about my day?"

Terri was used to customers like this. They were a real pain in the ass and always left a bitter taste in her mouth, but most of the time the customers at least wrote down their full, legal name and phone number.

"Tell you what, why don't you just write your name and phone number, sign on the bottom, and when you have more time, call me and we can finish—"

"Fine!" the woman yelled. Terri snapped her head to see if Amanda was listening, but she was too busy helping Carla to care about the lady and her behavior. She began to rant as she picked up the pen and filled the paper out. "All I wanted to do was donate this shit my sister left behind – stupid woman, if you ask me; no clue where she ran off to this time – and go on with my day. But no. That's *never* how things work!"

She slammed the pen down, causing the pen cover to fly down to the floor. "But you know what? This is it. I've had it with her!"

This was definitely a woman you didn't want to fuck with. Terri attempted a smile, but as soon as she did, the woman ran out of the store. At least she had the paperwork and could move on. She hoped that this woman would never come back to her store. The woman was not someone she would want around her customers, especially the disabled woman who stopped in with her caregiver.

She happened to look inside the haphazardly packed box. Sitting inside the corner of the box was a gorgeous stuffed dog. Pulling it out, she grinned. The stuffed dog had two blue-button eyes barely an inch apart from each other and a goofy grin painted on its face. It wasn't the original features of the dog that caught her attention the most – rather, it was the small, red ribbon tied to its paw that sent her.

This was the perfect gift for a perfect baby girl!

-2-

She couldn't wait for Christmas. Terri loved everything about the holiday, especially giving gifts and seeing the reaction from her daughter when she saw the present awaiting her. Terri was notorious for hiding things well—too well, according to her ex—and took advantage of this talent every year. It didn't matter how hard Amanda would look, or even how hard Jeff would look when he tried to find his birthday present. They could never find their gifts without some kind of help from her. She hid them too well.

Terri took weird pleasure in seeing them frustrated and irritated as they would go through the house to find their gifts. One year, Jeff and Amanda teamed up together and made a big mess as they furiously searched for their presents. The best gift that year was them also cleaning their mess together. She sat on the couch and sipped on a glass of red wine, reveling in the fact she didn't have to clean up after them!

Yeah, it was never a typical holiday. She had made it a tradition – instead of placing gifts under some tree that would take up too much space, she would do treasure hunts. Amanda loved it, but Jeff? Not so much. He always complained, so she stopped with Jeff but kept the magic alive for her daughter.

She could hear a car heading into the driveway and knew that he was on his way to pick up Amanda. She hated it. Why couldn't she have full custody of Amanda?

"Because you're a lez," that horrible man said in her mind's ear. "The state believes that a healthy child should be raised by normal people, and you aren't normal. But that doesn't mean she can't visit – she just can't live in the same house with you." She recalled telling the lawyer to go screw himself. He laughed right in her face.

Terri could hear Jeff knocking on the door, in that annoying hard way he would do. Four or five really hard slams on the door and she opened the door.

Jeff was a very attractive man. He stood a few inches taller than her, his biceps looking like they were about to rip his shirt. With all that muscle he had now, she no longer wondered why he got into that fitness kick after their divorce. Not that he wasn't attractive before, but she missed his beer belly.

"She ready to go?" Jeff spoke, his baritone voice indicating he didn't want to stick around for a long time.

"Almost. I'll go check."

"Terri," Jeff said as she turned. He touched her shoulder, making her close her eyes in annoyance.

"What?"

"This is silly. What happened to us?"

Terri couldn't believe what she was hearing. "What do you mean by that?"

"I mean, this weird phase you're going through. That woman living here. I know you don't love her the way you loved me."

Terri laughed, almost maliciously. "You're right, Jeff Toms. I don't love her the way I loved you. I love her more."

Jeff scoffed. "Really? You love a woman more than you love a man? Please."

Terri had enough of this horse shit. "Every week! Every damn week, you come in here, say something cruel about

Delana or about me. I'd like to know what you tell that woman you've shacked with."

"She puts out better than you did with me," Jeff began, but stopped when he saw Amanda coming out of the kitchen with Delana. He immediately frowned; his lips pursed in disgust.

"Hi, Jeff," Delana said, almost too cheerily. "Amanda's been a great little girl—"

"I'd like it if you kept your hands off her, Delana," he retorted, deliberately saying her name wrong. "If I had it my way—"

Terri cut him off, completely ignoring his bullshit. "You got everything?" she asked her daughter.

"Yes, Mommy," replied Amanda. Jeff reached out a hand for his daughter's overnight bag. Delana intentionally dropped the bag to the ground, making Jeff pick it up. He met her eyes very briefly and took Amanda's hand.

And just like that, Jeff's demeanor changed completely.

"Baby girl!" he exclaimed as he lifted her up and put her on his shoulders. "You ready to go home?"

In response, Amanda giggled.

"I'll see you in a few days, honey," Terri said to her daughter as they turned and left the house, doing the best she could to hold it together before closing the door.

She turned to Delana and began to cry. Delana hugged her tight. She wasn't sure if Terri was crying because of that douchebag, or if she already missed her daughter.

Or maybe it was both. She could never tell.

WHEN THEY WALKED into Jeff's small two-bedroom house, Ida was reclining at the couch, flipping through the channels. Amanda greeted her, but Ida ignored the girl. Jeff hardly noticed, taking Amanda's overnight bag into his daughter's room, dropping the bag on her bed. She began to remove the contents of the bag and placed her toys where she liked having them.

Ida appeared in the doorway and lit up a cigarette. She was a short woman, but her height didn't keep her from standing tall over anyone, regardless of their size. Wearing a wrinkled, graphic t-shirt which screamed her rock and roll personality, she folded her thick arms as the cigarette rested on her thick, pink lips. She watched the little girl with contempt. She wondered why the brat couldn't stay with her biological mother. She did not mind one bit Terri was a lesbian, and actually sided with Terri for having full custody, but it was not of a selfless manner.

"How many more of these things do you need?" she asked as she took out the long cigarette from her lips, puffing out a cloud of smoke into the room. "Aren't you getting a bit old for these useless toys?"

"They aren't useless," Amanda protested. "They're family."

"Family, huh?" Ida smirked, eyeing the stupid collection practically hiding Amanda's pillows. "Tell me, what kind of family are they, besides being stuffed with cotton?"

Amanda wasn't sure how to respond. She nervously arranged the stuffed animals in a way that would have impressed her biological mother. "A family that loves and cares for each other."

"Stupid girl," Ida sneered and snatched one of the animals. Her cigarette was dangerously close to the stuffed bear. "They are inanimate. Do you know what that means?"

"Inanimate?"

"They can't move. They can't speak. They can't care and love for each other!"

"But they do!"

In a moment of pure malice, she pressed the tip of the cigarette to the stuffed bear Amanda received five weeks ago. "Oh no, look what happened to the dumb bear!"

Amanda was petrified. Her jaw fell down in complete shock. She couldn't even manage to respond to at what she had just witnessed.

"Close your mouth," she snapped as she wiped the glaring burn mark on the toy. "It's a toy. A toy that doesn't move. Doesn't breathe. It's a toy."

"What is that smell?" Jeff demanded, walking into the room. He happened to see the bear in Ida's hand, her cigarette between her fingers.

Her voice completely changed; her cruel tone had replaced itself with ingenuine sorrow. "It was my fault, Jeff. I was just admiring this stuffed animal – you know, it reminded me so much of the one I had when I was Amanda's age, and my cigarette hit it. I'm sorry!" Ida cried out in fake tears. "I'm such a klutz!"

"You have to be more careful, dear. Give me the toy. I'll have to throw it away."

Amanda knew better than to say anything. She wanted desperately to tell her dad just how awful and horrible her stepmother was, but she knew if she did, another yelling match would happen. She hated yelling.

Worse of all, Jeff never believed her anyway. It was just better to remain quiet. She could tell her real mom about how awful Ida was, but that wouldn't do any good either. She would just tell Jeff and the same result would happen.

"Christmas is around the corner, honey," he said as he neared the door to leave. "I'm sure you'll get more toys. I know nothing can replace Steve Stuffingtons, but sometimes accidents happen."

"Yeah, dear. Accidents happen," Ida said, still not feeling any remorse at all. "Why don't you go play outside? It's nice out."

"Good idea," Jeff replied. "You can make a snowman or something."

WITHIN JUST A few minutes of playing outside, Amanda decided to make a snowman, as her dad had suggested. As she began making the first part of its body, she heard someone approach her from behind.

"Hi," the child said. "I'm Violet. But you can call me Vi. A lot of people call me that."

Amanda turned and smiled. "I'm Amanda."

"Are you making a snowperson?" Violet asked her.

"I'm not very good," Amanda said, grinning.

"That's okay. It doesn't have to be really good; you know."

"I guess," she said in agreement. She looked down at Violet's wrist. She wasn't wearing any gloves and had a red ribbon tied to her dark-skinned wrist, as though it was a bracelet. She had light blue eyes and her hair was long, ruined by the wind. She seemed really nice and friendly.

For the next few minutes, they worked together to create an imperfect, small snowman. Both of them laughed as they finished putting on the finishing touches of the creation. Vi turned to Amanda. "What should we name it?"

"You did a lot of the work," Amanda said. "Let's call it Violet."

"But it's your house," Violet said pointedly. "It should bear your name."

Amanda didn't like that idea. She thought about a name for the snowman and smiled. "I'll call it Sunny Snowman."

"It melts at the name," Vi said, laughing.

"It's dumb, isn't it?"

"No, I was just being silly. I like that name."

Amanda smiled. "Where do your parents live? Maybe you can stay around for supper?"

Vi frowned. "I don't think they'd like that too much."

"Oh, okay," Amanda said, frowning too. She liked her and wanted to keep hanging out with Vi.

"I'm just visiting my aunt. She taught me a really cool poem. Wanna hear it?"

"Sure!" Amanda's face lightened up a bit more.

"It's kinda creepy, but I like how it sounds. You ready?"

"Uh huh!"

"Okay. Here it goes." The girl took a deep breath before she began to recite the poem from memory. Just as she opened her mouth, she looked over at one of the houses down the street. "Actually, I'll have to tell you later."

"But I wanna hear the poem!"

The front door opened. Jeff stood inside, watching his little girl play. It was time to come inside, he told her.

Amanda turned around to tell her friend goodbye, but Vi had disappeared from sight. "Weird," she murmured.

I didn't even hear her leave.

-3-

Movie nights were probably one of the best times of the week for Amanda. It was a tradition first started by Jeff when Terri was pregnant with their daughter. He knew that Terri didn't really care for the movie – after all, most of the time watching movies was spent snuggling and kissing on the couch rather than actually watching *The Fuller Brush Girl* or some quirky 70's comedy Terri particularly liked.

When Amanda grew older – Jeff was certain Amanda was three years old – the movies changed so that Amanda could also watch them. There was something quite nostalgic about putting in *The Aristocats* and *Bedknobs and Broomsticks.* He loved those movies, so when Amanda wanted to watch those movies over and over again, Jeff never put up a fight. Terri soon stopped watching the films and would pull out one of her thrillers or a magazine instead of watching with them. At first, Jeff wanted Terri to join in on the family fun time, but she was at least doing her part by being in the room.

Tonight, the movie of choice was *The Wizard of Oz.* It was his absolute favorite movie, and he grew up reading the fourteen-book series. From time to time, he would approach the beautiful oak wood bookshelf sitting in the living room and pull out one of the fourteen books and read a few chapters, just to escape from the harsh reality he now had to face on a daily basis. Normally, if Ida was present, he would have to force himself to watch her movies – movies Jeff absolutely couldn't stand.

About forty-five minutes into the movie, Jeff looked over at his daughter, her eyes practically glued to the television set. "You like this time we have together, don't you?"

Amanda nodded. "I like watching movies with you."

"Do you wish you were living with your mom, instead of living here?" He didn't know why he asked the question, but it was burning inside of him for a few days.

"When Other Mom isn't here, I do," she murmured, but Jeff heard her loud and clear.

"What do you mean?"

"She's mean to me."

"Mean? How?"

"She says mean things to me. She calls me dumb and stupid and other things."

Jeff was bothered by this. He loved Ida but listening to his daughter talk about her like this was upsetting. "She hasn't spent a lot of time with you, I know."

"I don't want her to," Amanda said, suppressing a yawn.

"But you really should," Jeff urged.

"But what if she says something mean to me again?"

Jeff was quiet for a couple minutes, distracted by the sound of the munchkins reveling in a happy funeral dirge. "I'll talk with her. She shouldn't be saying mean things to you."

"But what if she doesn't listen to you?"

"I'm sure she will," Jeff said, not believing the bullshit coming out of his mouth. She was a tough one, and he knew why she was like the way she was. Ida had always been a force to be reckoned with – it was this very trait about her that attracted him to the woman who took Terri's place. She could be boisterous and to-the-point. Rather authoritarian.

They had met at a party when he was close to finalizing the divorce. She was loud and put some idiotic guy in his place when he attempted to slap her in the ass. Jeff saw red – you just don't do that kind of thing! He grabbed the guy at the collar of his disgusting polo that was way too small for him in the first place and came close to punching him in the face. But Ida grabbed Jeff before he could throw the punch.

"Yeah, thanks for that, but I'm a tough bitch and would have done what you were planning on doing," she remarked when the guy walked away.

"It's just not right to treat a beautiful woman like the way he treated you," Jeff replied, grabbing his Rob Roy from the table. "Makes my skin crawl."

"You're reactive," she mused. "I find that very sexy."

"Oh?"

"Yeah. Oh," Ida laughed, accidentally snorting. Jeff couldn't help but laugh, despite trying his damndest to hold it back.

They spent a good two hours just talking. They had a lot in common, having similar experiences when they were teenagers. Both of them were suspended from school for their reactive behaviors and tried hashish for the first time during their first semester at their respective colleges.

It wasn't Jeff who wanted to sleep with her, but Ida put the first move and they ended up fucking the night away. They married three months later. Ida knew about Amanda early on, and she seemed very thrilled at the prospect of raising a little girl, but as time went on, Jeff couldn't help but notice she wasn't the same person when Amanda was around.

And he hated himself for it – one moment, he wanted his daughter to live with him every single day of the week and not have to share custody. But another moment, he would prefer to save this second marriage from falling apart. He knew damn well if Amanda lived with her biological mother full-time, Ida would be back to her normal self.

Or maybe this was her normal self.

The thought scared him.

Amanda yawned. Jeff looked over at his daughter and once again, weighed the cost of both choices. No. Ida would have to grin and bear it for as long as possible. *He* would have to grin and bear it for as long as possible. "Getting tired, sweetheart?"

She nodded.

"We can finish this movie tomorrow, if you want."

"Okay."

Jeff stopped the movie and turned the television off. He was also getting rather tired, even though it wasn't exactly ten in the evening. Ida had not come home yet from her night out with her friends, and he knew when she did, she would be drunk as a skunk.

HE AWOKE TO the sound of someone crashing into the wall. Getting up out of bed slowly, he opened his bedroom door and saw Ida on the floor, laughing to herself, one of the framed pictures of their honeymoon on the ground. It reminded him of that disturbing scene from *The Evil Dead.* He closed his eyes in irritation.

"Come on, honey. You—"

"Honey. I'm suh-weet like honey, right?" Ida laughed again, and she was being louder than normal.

"Yes, of course—"

"Honey rolls."

Confused, but knowing better than to encourage this behavior, he reached over to grab Ida by the arm, in a faint attempt to bring her to bed. She slapped his arm away.

"Don't you touch me! DON'T YOU FUCKIN' TOUCH ME!" she shrieked.

Jeff turned around, the sound of another door opening catching his attention.

Fuck me.

"Daddy?" said Amanda groggily. He began to walk over to her, but Ida grabbed him by the leg.

"No, no you fuckin' don't!" she continued to yell at him.

"Go back to bed, sweetheart, okay? Please?" he urged Amanda. She couldn't help but stare at the drunken woman lying on the floor.

"That's a fittin' term for that thing. Sweethearts are disgusting, AND SO ARE YOU!" she cried out in Amanda's direction as her door closed. Jeff could hear his daughter crying in her room. It broke his heart.

Then something surged inside of him, as though he was the toaster in the kitchen being plugged into the wall, the electricity resurrecting the kitchen appliance. He broke free of Ida's clutches. Entering the room, Jeff stopped as he closed the door, locking it behind him. It was a moment like this where he didn't feel so weirded out by the lock on the door. He was surprised Amanda didn't press on the lock when she ran back into her room.

"Get dressed, and quickly, okay?" Jeff said as he grabbed her bookbag from the chair and stuffed a few night's worth of clothes inside.

Tears in her eyes, she nodded and hurried to get dressed. When she was finished, he scooped her up in his arms. "Daddy, where are we going?"

"You'll find out," he whispered to her.

IT WAS CLOSE to 2:30 in the morning when he approached Terri's house. He knew there was an eighty percent chance they were still awake – fondling each other, more than likely – so he didn't have to knock for long when the door was opened. But it wasn't Terri who answered the door.

"Sup?" a very tired Delana spoke, wiping her eyes.

"Where's Terri?"

"In bed, sleeping, just like I was doing a second ago before you pounded on the door at three in the morning."

"Wake her up. Please, Delana."

"Did something happen?" Terri asked as she ambled into the room, buttoning up her pajamas.

"Your ex is here, your daughter in tow," replied Delana, taking Amanda carefully out of Jeff's burly arms.

"I can see that," Terri said, her brows arching into a look of confusion.

"Ida's beyond drunk," Jeff said as Delana left the two alone, bringing Amanda into her bedroom.

"Shit," Terri whispered. "Did anything…" she trailed off, too angry to say anything further.

Jeff sunk into the couch, his elbows on his legs and his hands covering his face. She sat down next to him.

"Please, Jeff. Did she do anything to our daughter?"

"She's been verbally abusing our daughter."

As though Terri took a large drink of the strongest coffee she could drink, she jolted awake.

"That fucking—"

"I'm livid."

Then Terri turned her head over to him, and he regretted moving his hands away from his eyes. There was new makeup on her face – a vibrant red mixed in with hues of blue.

"This is what you exposed our daughter to: a loathsome motherfucking cunt?" she hissed at him. "Get the hell out of here! GET OUT!"

Jeff pleaded with his ex-wife with his eyes. "Amanda's heard so much shouting tonight. Some of which was directed toward her. We need to remain calm and cool. Please, Terri."

She soon regretted her childish – yet much-needed – outburst. Sighing, she collected herself together, as difficult as the task was. "Of course. I am going to hate myself for asking, but what is she saying to her?"

"Dumb. Stupid. You know she hates Sweethearts because they're too sweet for her?"

"What?"

"I tried to calm Amanda down and called her sweetheart.

Then Ida replied back. 'Sweethearts are disgusting, and so are you.' I should have punched her."

"And Amanda would've seen all that," Terri said to herself.

"And it wouldn't have been right to do so," Jeff added. "And now we're here."

Terri wondered what the best thing would be to do. She looked over at Jeff, her eyes fading back to their former tired selves. She looked up at the ceiling as she spoke. "Amanda's staying here for the time being. I think that's best."

"I'll get a motel for a couple nights," Jeff said.

"No," Terri replied, surprising herself. "Stay here for the night. You can take the couch."

"Are you absolutely sure?"

Terri wasn't absolutely sure, to be quite honest. "As soon as you wake up, we're going over to your house and getting a couple things I know you probably forgot to pack. I haven't done her laundry yet and I'm too fucking tired to do her clothes right now. Plus, I have some words I want to say to that bitch."

IT WAS THE moment both of them were dreading. It took Jeff a long time to get ready, and Terri was acting the same way. As they finished their morning coffee, they left in Jeff's car. The ride to Jeff's place was long and quiet – almost too quiet for Terri's liking, but one cup of coffee just wasn't really waking her up.

When they finally parked in the driveway, Jeff told Terri to wait in the car until he gave her the go-ahead to leave the car. He walked over to the door and went in.

About thirty seconds later, Jeff left and motioned for Terri to come in. She figured Ida was not home, so she wouldn't have to confront her.

Instead, she was greeted with a harsh "what?" by Ida, who was lying on the couch, smoking a cigarette. Ashes were falling all over the floor – something Terri would not have allowed in her house. She couldn't help but think how slovenly Ida was. It made her hate the bitch even more.

"Let's go and pack up some of Amanda's things," Jeff whispered.

"You don't need to whisper," Ida croaked out. "I heard you."

Terri tried her best to compose herself, but the part wanting to release left her. "I'm glad you heard him," Terri hissed at Ida. "How dare you attack my daughter!"

"Oh calm down, you dyke," Ida retorted.

"Don't you talk to me like that!" Terri screamed.

"Come on, Terri. Let's get Amanda's things—"

"No need for that," Ida interrupted. "You'll find her shit on the floor in the hallway.

Jeff couldn't stop what was happening before his eyes. Terri barreled over to Ida and smacked her across the face. "You bitch! How dare you treat my daughter like a tattered rag doll! How dare you mistreat my daughter! What the fuck!"

Jeff rushed over to his ex-wife and pulled her back. "It's not worth it, Terri."

"She needs help, Jeff. Someone who can't even hold their own liquor and treats a child the way she does, needs help."

"You're right," Jeff said quietly.

"I don't need help," Ida hissed, her words dripping like vinegar in Jeff's ears. "I don't need help."

"Ida, please," Jeff said, sounding upset. "This isn't acceptable. Your constant drinking is probably hurting you physically than it is hurting me and Amanda. You need help."

"I. Don't. Like. Children," Ida said tonelessly, but the impact of the words were much more expressive than Jeff could have imagined.

"Is that why you're drinking?" Jeff asked her, while Terri went into Amanda's room and began taking as much as she could take with her.

"Maybe. Or maybe not. But I don't need help."

"Then it's over between us, Ida. I want you out of this house. I want you out of my life."

The weight of Jeff's words slapped her across the face like Terri had just done. She loved Jeff, but she didn't love Amanda. She didn't want her relationship with Jeff to end.

"No," she mumbled. Then her voice started to swell. "You can't do this. I won't allow it."

"I will not allow you to treat Amanda like shit anymore. I will not allow you to stay out all night and turn yourself into a violent mess. Enough is enough."

Ida got up from the couch and stared dumbly at Jeff. "You're right, Jeff. I need help."

Terri walked into the living room and glared at Ida. She spoke no words – the expression painted on her face was enough to tame a wild lion.

"Teresa," Ida started, "I'm sorry for what I've done. I really am."

"It's Terri," she hissed.

"Yeah. Terri. Right." A small smile creeped onto Ida's face. "I'm going to get some help. I can't do this anymore. I can't."

"I'm glad you are getting help, Ida," Terri said, but she didn't really believe what Ida was saying. She didn't trust Ida at all. "I hope you grow from this."

"I will, Teresa. I will." She moved around the room, straightening up her things and placing them gingerly into her purse.

Then she left the house, leaving Jeff and Terri in the room together, wondering if Ida will really go through with this, wondering if a woman like Ida could really grow and mature. Both of them wondered if Ida would really stop drinking and be a better influence on their daughter.

-4-

The next couple weeks were close to being completely peaceful. Since Ida had left Jeff's house and checked herself in at the nearby rehabilitation facility, Amanda seemed to have brightened up. Terri could see the impact of having Ida out of Jeff's house just by looking into her daughter's eyes. The oft repeated saying, "the eyes are the window to the soul" never before rang so true as they did in those weeks.

It was the way Amanda woke up in the morning. Amanda didn't seem as groggy as she normally did when Terri had her on the weekends. Her voice was even brighter than before. She seemed happier, seemed even more joyful than she was a few weeks ago.

It wasn't just the fact that Ida was out of Amanda's life playing a factor in Amanda's countenance – Christmas was only a day away. Any child would be excited and thrilled for Christmas. Terri remembered how she felt around this time of year, knowing that her parents had bought her toys. Granted, it was the few times her parents were able to buy gifts for her – Terri did not grow up swimming in pools of money, nor did she receive everything her childish heart desired. Her father scrounged the last couple weeks of the Christmas holiday to ensure Terri got something for the holiday, even longer when it came to her birthday.

Those gifts meant way more to her than receiving gifts from others. There was something about knowing the situation of her wealthier family members in contrast to the situation of her parents. They could buy those gifts any old time and give them to her. Her father couldn't do that. She could still imagine her father's eyes glisten, as though his eyes were gold underneath a hot July sun. Comparing her father's nonverbals to other family members was the driving force in not desiring great wealth. She saw what the love of money could do to others who were foolish with what they were given.

Delana woke up earlier than normal so she could begin preparing for Christmas morning breakfast. Terri remained still in bed, the smells of caramel rolls and the sound of sizzling bacon tempting her to leave her comfortable, soft bed. The scent of the lavender in the diffuser was fighting a sensual battle with the cooking.

But the smell of food ended up winning this battle. Terri slowly got out of bed, examining herself in the mirror. Yawning, she attempted to straighten out her hair by pulling it back. She thought about throwing herself in the shower, something to do while the food was still cooking.

Usually, Amanda was the one barging into the bedroom on Christmas day, dragging her out of bed and in front of the Christmas tree. But for some reason that wasn't making a lot of sense, Amanda didn't.

I really hope she didn't fall ill like she did four years ago, Terri thought to herself. The bedroom door was slightly ajar; she pulled it open and walked slowly out of the room, another smell taking her by surprise. It wasn't the bacon, nor was it the smell of caramel. It was something even more amazing, one she wasn't expecting at all.

"Delana, you didn't," Terri said, embracing her from behind, kissing Delana on the neck.

A soft laugh escaped Delana's lips. "Merry Christmas, babe."

"Mommy!" Amanda cried out. To Terri's relief, she noticed the mess of food all over Amanda's pajamas. She was clearly helping out in the kitchen. She obviously was not sick at all.

"Well, if this isn't a beautiful Christmas gift," Terri grinned. "You and Amanda making breakfast."

"It's so much fun!" replied her beautiful baby girl.

"Yes!" Delana laughed, turning away from the fruit bowl. She gave Amanda a high-five and mussed up her hair a bit. Amanda scrunched up her face – she hated that, but when Delana was done, she giggled.

Amanda giggled.

It was beyond anything Terri expected. In all the time she had spent with Delana, Amanda showed absolutely no interest in cooking. She showed absolutely no interest in food! And even more phenomenal, Amanda giggled after having someone mess up her hair!

This was huge.

"That tickled," she replied.

"Oh, did it?" Delana responded coyly, pretending to threaten Amanda's hair with the gravy-covered serving spoon on the counter.

"You wouldn't dare," Amanda said, her eyes narrowing. At first, Terri thought she was being serious, but then she grabbed a wooden spoon from the other side of the counter.

"This is war, little girl!" Delana said, grabbing the ladle. Amanda screamed, holding on to the wooden spoon for dear life. They played swords with the cooking utensils, gravy flying all over and landing on their pajamas. Terri couldn't help but laugh.

The moment certainly is a Kodak moment. She reveled in this silly moment. As they continued fighting, she didn't even flinch when a spot of gravy landed on her cheek. Instead, she wiped a finger on the assaulted cheek and gave it a taste. It was the best breakfast gravy she ever tasted!

Terri moaned in pleasure. "Please tell me breakfast is

about to be served in a few minutes."

"Give or take about five to six minutes," Delana replied back as she washed her spoon. Amanda set down her weapon and went to hug Terri.

"Merry Christmas, mommy!" she said, grabbing Terri's leg and looking up at her.

"Merry Christmas, sweetie. Are you having fun cooking?"

Instead of saying anything, Amanda grinned and nodded. Yup, it confirmed everything Terri knew about Delana – she must be a magician! "What did you do to my daughter?" she asked Delana teasingly, while Amanda went back to what she was doing.

She laughed. "I have no idea. I woke up early, just threw the rolls in the oven, and then all of a sudden, this little gem was in the kitchen with me! She wanted something to do, so I let her help me with a couple things."

"You did something I never expected, and succeeded," Terri whispered. "I think I'm in love with you – no wait, I AM in love with you!"

Once again, the two embraced and kissed. Amanda covered her eyes, as she normally would do, and groaned. "Gross!"

"I need to get the camera!" exclaimed Terri. She rushed into the living room and grabbed the camera on the shelf. Amanda was still helping out with Delana, so she took the moment and captured it on film.

"Can you two get a bit closer, as though you're stirring the gravy together?" Delana and Amanda complied. Delana grabbed the middle of the spoon, Amanda settling hers right above Delana's hand. They looked up at her and smiled.

"I love it!" Terri cried out while she took another picture, reveling in the moment.

"Okay, everything is very close to being done. Honey, can you go get cleaned up and get dressed, then we can eat our breakfast?" asked Delana to Amanda.

"Okay!"

She rushed out of the kitchen and into her bedroom. Terri stayed behind, watching her little girl. She was growing up. She wanted every moment to be like this: joyful, loving, exciting.

"I'd better get cleaned up, too," she murmured. She happened to notice a bit of gravy on her pajama shirt.

A flash took her by surprise. Delana held the camera, smiling wickedly at Terri. "You know, you don't get an out when it comes to Kodak moments."

Terri laughed. "No, I suppose I don't."

Delana grabbed Terri by her hips and kissed her again. Terri could feel herself getting excited – seeing Delana in the kitchen, looking sexy and wearing that silly apron over her blue pajamas and holding the ladle was enough for her to burst out of her skin.

"I've got a gift for you, but you can't open it until much later tonight," Terri whispered in Delana's ear, making her point by sticking her tongue in Delana's ear. She groaned.

"But I want it now," Delana purred, her fingers lightly caressing Terri's sides.

"The waiting might be treacherous," Terri replied slyly, "but it will be very much worth it."

IT WAS EXTREMELY difficult to be motivated to do anything after such a heavy breakfast. Between bites of caramel rolls, biscuits and gravy, eggs, bacon, and freshly cut fruit, Terri wanted to do nothing at all. Delana and Terri stared at each other, as though waiting for each other to burst from all the food they had consumed.

Terri was the first person to say anything after the meal. "My God, that was the best breakfast I've ever eaten. And I hardly eat breakfast."

Delana groaned. "I think I ate enough for the rest of the day."

"I say let's go back to bed, and just lay down."

"Mommy!" Amanda cried out. "It's Christmas! We just got out of bed!"

Terri laughed softly. "We're just kidding, baby girl. Give us a couple minutes and we'll be out in the living room, opening our gifts."

Amanda got up from the table, giving her mothers a stern look, her small hands on her hips. "You have two minutes. Two minutes, okay?" Terri bit her lower lip to keep herself from laughing. She looked over at Delana – she was doing the same thing.

"Two minutes?" Delana said, sounding comically offended. "What about two hours?"

"Two minutes is two minutes," Amanda replied back, still sounding serious. She then walked out of the kitchen and into the living room.

The two women sitting at the table lost it. "We'd better get out there before Mom grounds us," Terri whispered, fake groaning as they got up from the table.

Delana choked back a laugh as Terri sat down on the couch next to Amanda. "My gifts first!" Delana said excitedly as she picked up two gifts from under the tree. Handing them over, she sat down next to Terri, watching them in absolute excitement.

It was night and day, watching the two open up the gifts. Terri was carefully unwrapping the gift, her fingers lightly touching the inside of the crease of the wrapping paper, pulling slowly. Delana knew she was teasing her, but she didn't mind. Amanda was like a tiger pouncing on its prey, getting to the box before Terri finally opened up hers.

"Mom! Hurry up!" Amanda cried, holding in the temptation to grab her mother's gift and open it for her. "You're taking, like, forever!"

"Patience is a virtue," Terri said gently, finally getting to the box.

"Not on Christmas," Amanda retorted back. Terri could only laugh – her daughter was right. It was Christmas and she could sense the annoyance in her partner's eyes when she was unwrapping the box. She lived for it.

"Now you can open the boxes," Delana said, getting up to prepare herself to get her present. She knew Terri had set up a quest to find theirs, and Delana was getting even more antsy to find her present. She couldn't wait much longer.

"Oh, honey," Terri said, her right hand slowly reaching over her pink-painted lips. "Oh, honey."

Inside the box was a beautiful silver bracelet, both of their first names engraved on the plate. Two golden hearts bordered their names on each side. She could sense a few tears coming down her face. Reaching over to the end-table for a tissue, Delana beat her to it, wiping the tears from her cheeks. "I love you, babe," Delana said quietly, softly kissing Terri on the lips.

Amanda was just as happy with her gift as Terri was. It wasn't a stuffed animal, but it was something even more precious. Terri looked at Delana and smiled knowingly. She had some input on this gift, knowing fully well that Amanda would cherish it.

It was a small, personalized statue of a little girl holding a toy, one that Delana had commissioned to have done for a very decent price. Her brother, Matt, was a talented artist who had a successful sculpting company in Philadelphia and was more than happy to do this for her. Out of everyone else in the Burton family, he was the one who didn't scorn at her for her life choices. Matt wanted his sister to be happy, but her parents and younger sister had different feelings.

That's what you get when your family is brought up in a strict Catholic home. To this day, driving past a Catholic church brought back bad memories of her childhood. In the beginning, it was much worse.

"Thanks, Mom!" Amanda jumped off the couch and gave her one of her big hugs. Delana kissed her on the forehead – that was probably the best gift anyone could receive, to be acknowledged as a parent even though you weren't fully flesh and blood.

She nearly squeezed the life out of Amanda. Hearing this little child call her such an intimate, personal name made her burst in emotion. "I love you, kiddo."

"Okay, now it's Terri's turn," said one of the most attractive women in the room. "I have hidden your presents in various places in this home. It is your mission to find those gifts in under five minutes. Who's ready?"

"Are you ready, Mom?"

Good lord, if this girl keeps this up, I'm gonna be an emotional rollercoaster.

Delana replied back, "I'm so ready for this!"

Terri started to count down from five. As soon as she reached that magical number, both of them rushed out of the room, nearly tearing apart the whole place looking for their Christmas gifts.

Within a minute of the hunt, Jeff had arrived at their front door, knocking in the same, rough fashion as he normally did. He was holding gifts in his arms, but they dropped out of his grip when Terri let him in and gave him a hug.

"Holy fuck. I wasn't expecting that from you," Jeff said, doing nothing to hold back his shock.

"It's Christmas, Jeff," Terri replied back, smiling. "Consider that your gift."

"Because you didn't get me anything, did you?"

Terri smirked. "Honestly, I would have, but most of the month's money went to buying gifts for our daughter and Delana."

Jeff laughed. "In other words, you didn't really bother."

"Not really," she said honestly.

"It's okay, I really don't need anything anyway," he responded, trying to hide his disappointment. At the same time, he was grateful to not be a part of the Christmas Hunt. He knew better, but Terri was one of the best gift-givers he had ever met. He had never met anyone like her before. "Umm, I hope… Amanda wasn't the only person I brought a gift for."

Terri looked at him curiously. "You know, you don't have to get me anything."

"I know that," Jeff said, trying not to snap. It would have ruined the surprisingly good mood from her, and he didn't want to be a Scrooge. "But the last two weeks had me thinking about everything, and I feel like a complete jackass for how I treat Delana—"

"Seriously, you think you can hide the gift you got me in the bathroom?" Delana came from out of the hallway, holding a wrapped gift in her hand. "You know that's the one place in the house where I spend the most time in. Well, besides the kitchen, of course."

"Well next year, I'll have to hide it in the utility closet," Terri joked.

"Next year, that's going to be the first place I look," Delana retorted, looking at Jeff. "Merry Christmas, Jeff."

"Merry Christmas, Delana," he replied.

"Wow, you actually said my name correctly. Today is certainly a day of firsts, isn't it?"

"Umm, Delana?" Jeff asked, nervously shifting his feet.

"Umm, yeah?"

"I uh, I was at the Macy's, and…" he trailed off. He looked over at Terri, as though she was the gatekeeper of his words. "I got you something. I hope that's okay."

Delana and Terri exchanged amused glances.

"You bought me something?" Delana asked, intrigued.

Jeff handed over a small box. Delana took the gift slowly. Just as Delana was about to unwrap the gift, Terri called out to Amanda. "Hey, kiddo. What's taking you so long?"

Silence.

"I'll be right back. And if that gift is what I think it might be, I think we're gonna have to sit down and have a talk," Terri teased, leaving the room.

"Like that would ever happen," Delana murmured.

"Hmm?"

"Nothing," Delana replied hastily.

They were quiet for about thirty seconds before Jeff broke the silence. "It won't bite you. Go on, open it."

"I wanna wait for them."

"Between you and me, I kinda get antsy on Christmas day, having to wait to open gifts. I never cared for Terri's Christmas tradition."

"I think it makes the holiday even more fun," Delana replied, sounding a bit too defensive than she intended. "But, if you want me to open your gift now, I guess I could…" she said as she found her fingers fumbling around the paper. She was hesitant to open it at first, but once her fingers began the Dance of the Unwrapping, she couldn't help herself.

Delana eyed the gift curiously. She wasn't sure what to make of it, but she couldn't help but appreciate Jeff in that moment. "Umm…"

"I'm sorry – I'm not that great with gifts, and I didn't know what to get you – I mean, if it's inapp—"

"No, not at all," Delana responded back. "I mean, it's not something I'd expect from you, but it's not that inappropriate. At all."

"Are you saying that you like it?"

"I have a feeling this gift is more about what it symbolizes than its utility," she said slowly. "And now I feel like I should have gotten you something."

"I'm sorry, Delana. During those first couple months, I felt betrayed and felt like the love I had with Terri was fake, as though she wore a different costume during our marriage. I didn't realize it until Ida put herself in treatment, but the love she expresses with you is so different, much more meaningful.

"I guess what I'm saying is that I was not the one to make her happy – it was always going to be you. She restrained herself for so long, and when you listen to her story, you can see why. I know you can't just forgive me with the snap of your fingers but know that I am very sorry for the way I've treated you."

Delana was silent for a few seconds. She cleared her throat. "To be fair, you didn't even know about me until you walked into the bathroom when you got home that afternoon."

"The one and only time I didn't call when I left work," he smirked at Delana, winking at her. She couldn't help but let out a slight giggle.

"The one and only time you got sick from a tuna sandwich," she retorted.

Both of them started laughing.

"Shit, I don't even know why I let myself eat that disgusting convenience store sandwich!" Jeff replied, wiping tears coming down his eyes.

"Looks like someone's having a moment," they heard Terri say, as she headed into the living room.

"Just sharing some laughs," said Delana, gently rubbing away the tears of amusement rolling down her face.

Terri asked curiously, "What did Jeff get you?"

Delana held up the cigarette lighter. It reminded Terri of one you would find at a liberal California gas station – the lighter was brightly decorated, the colors of the rainbow decorating the front.

"Jeff, Delana doesn't smoke," said Terri, shaking her head.

"It's not about the lighter itself, but what it represents," Jeff explained.

"But Delana doesn't smoke," Terri pursued.

"Terri, sweetie, I like it. Am I going to use it? No, but I like it. That's all that matters."

Terri sighed. "I guess you're right." She turned around. "I gotta pee – I'll be right back."

As soon as Terri was out of earshot, she whispered to Jeff. "But I used to," Delana said.

"But you don't anymore?"

"Not since I met Terri," she answered.

For some reason, sharing this fact about her life with Jeff felt good. It felt almost like a stone was lifted off her shoulders. Delana continued to fumble around with the lighter. As each second passed, she found herself appreciating the man who should have held on to his unforgiveness, who should have hated her for the rest of his life but chose not to.

TERRI HAD HIDDEN Amanda's gift in a rather unique place in her room. She took extra care to ensure that the present was perfectly hidden in the growing clothes hamper in Amanda's room. It was perfect. Amanda always threw her clothes on the floor, and it would either be Terri or Delana who would give up on getting Amanda to clean up after herself and pick up the dirty clothes.

But Amanda was a smart cookie. While it was not the first place Amanda looked, she gave up looking for her present in the closet. She gave up looking for the present in her mothers' room. Suddenly, she heard her mom call out for her and she accidentally knocked the clothes hamper over. She saw something she didn't recognize in the basket.

She reached in and pulled out a beautifully wrapped, medium-sized box and shook it. It didn't make any noise, piquing her interest even more. She was really tempted to open the gift.

That little voice her mom called the conscience told her to just open it. To not wait. She let a small grin come over her face.

I think I will.

She began to unwrap the present. Right when she was close to the actual gift, her mom knocked on the door and immediately came into the room. Terri frowned at her daughter.

"Honey!" she exclaimed. "Come on – let's go into the living room. You can finish opening your gift with us. Your

Dad's here!"

Amanda regretted opening the gift. She apologized as they left the room and joined the adults. Her dad gave her a really big hug and a kiss on the forehead as he handed over the gift he had brought for her.

"Well guess who tried to be sneaky and open their gift in private?" Terri teased, winking at her daughter. "It's all right though – you still don't know what it is."

"The apple doesn't fall far from the family tree," Jeff laughed, giving his daughter a wink as well.

"You're right – you're just as impatient as your daughter," Terri rolled her eyes. She gestured for her family to start opening their gifts. She loved the chaos of seeing both of them rip the paper off and reveled in the sound of paper being torn.

Amanda was the first one (no surprises there) to get to her gift. She looked at the stuffed dog tucked in the box and gasped.

Score!

"I love her!" the little girl exclaimed to her mom.

"Got a name for her?" asked Terri.

Amanda scrunched up her face, like she always did when pondering what to call her stuffed animals. She looked at the little puppy, taking special note of the little blue-button eyes. She glanced at the red ribbon tied to its paw, gently touching it. She could feel it warmly pulsing on the tip of her thumb.

"Violet Red," she murmured.

Delana asked her, "What did you say, sweetie?"

Amanda was quiet for several seconds. "Her name is Violet Red."

Terri looked at her daughter in surprise. She expected her daughter to use the Stuffingtons surname. The fact Amanda departed from naming her animals a common first name with the surname associated with it was a first. Every single stuffed animal, right from the large panda bear sitting in the corner of her room to the small piglet on her headboard was a part of this Stuffingtons family.

Jeff asked his daughter, "Why Violet Red?"

"I don't know," she said quietly. "It just came to me."

Delana asked if she could see the dog for a second. At first, Amanda was hesitant. She didn't want anyone handling the toy, but she knew if she said no, she would get scolded. She handed it over to her mom.

"It's a really cute name," she said. "I love it." Delana repeated the name.

Amanda was getting nervous. And anxious as Delana continued to check the toy out. She wanted Violet Red back! Something inside of her demanded for Amanda to hold the toy. She tried as hard as she could to restrain herself from snatching Violet Red out of Delana's hand.

She could feel her hand darting over to the toy and grabbed it out of Delana's hand.

"Amanda!" Terri cried. "We don't do that kind of thing! You apologize to your mom, now, young lady!"

She looked at Delana apologetically. "I didn't mean to do that," she whispered. "I'm sorry."

Delana smiled weakly. "It's okay," she replied. "I was very protective of my stuffed animal collection too, when I was your age."

Amanda smiled back. She set the dog aside and gave Delana a hug. She didn't mean to do what she did.

Or did she? Amanda couldn't help wondering.

WITH THE CHRISTMAS morning all said and done, the rest of the day was spent at home, for the most part. Terri, Delana, and Jeff spent a couple hours in the house, drinking coffee and talking about how things were going with Ida. Jeff said she was making great progress, and Ida was going to be coming back to his place.

"I don't think she should be near Amanda," said Delana, finishing her cup of coffee, reaching for the carafe to refill her mug.

"I agree," Terri replied. "What if Ida relapses?"

Jeff couldn't help but disagree with the women. He had seen remarkable progress, a change in Ida's whole demeanor. She was much happier, and she even said she was excited to see Amanda again. For a moment, Jeff thought she was lying, but the way her eyes were lightening up indicated she was ending her ill will toward Amanda.

"I don't think she will. I really don't."

"It's ultimately your decision on what you want to do moving forward," Terri said. "But if God forbid anything happens from this point forward, I will have to move Amanda here permanently."

"I don't blame ya," Jeff responded. "But I really think Ida has turned a whole new leaf."

"If you say so," Terri murmured.

Jeff ended up leaving the house thirty minutes later, leaving the women in the living room. They were silent for a few minutes before Delana suggested turning on the television to watch her favorite Christmas film. Terri wasn't a big fan of *A Christmas Carol.* She hated the story for some reason – it was probably her English teacher that ruined the movie for her. Having to write a paper about the differences between the novella and the film drove her crazy.

Despite her dislike of the movie, Delana slipped the VHS into the VCR and they ended up watching the film. She snuggled up next to Terri, the smell of Terri's faint lavender-perfumed hair comforting her.

"I love that smell," she murmured in Terri's ear. She smiled. "It sends me."

"You flirt," Terri laughed softly. "Everything sends you."

Within seconds, they began to make out in front of the television set, paying no attention to the screen. Terri reclined back, letting Delana move her hands gently against the side of her body.

"Right there, yes," Terri whispered, closing her eyes. A

soft groan came out of her lips while Delana crawled on top of her, kissing her neck and upper chest, her hands still caressing Terri's sides.

The sound of a thump coming from somewhere in the house caused them to pause their lovemaking. It sounded like something fell.

"What was that?" asked Delana.

"Dunno," Terri replied. "Don't stop, though."

They resumed kissing.

THUMP!

Now it sounded like something was falling in the hallway. Terri gently took Delana aside and got up, curious to know what had fallen. She noticed one of Delana's paintings had fallen off the shelf.

"Weird," she mumbled, picking up the framed artwork and positioning it against a couple hardbacks so that it wouldn't fall again. She heard her daughter talking in her room. She must be up from her nap.

She gently knocked on the door and walked in the room. Amanda was sitting on her bed, talking to her new toy. Immediately, the unique name Amanda had given the toy came into her head.

"Hey kiddo," she said, smiling. "You really do love that toy, don't you?"

Amanda replied with a soft, knowing smile. "She likes it here."

"Well, I'm glad for Violet Rose."

"Violet *Red*, mom," Amanda said, correcting her. "Violet Red."

"What made you think of that name?"

Amanda paused for a moment as she thought about how to respond. "I didn't."

"Well, it's a very sweet name," Terri replied. "But how come she's not one of the Stuffingtons?"

"She's different from them," Amanda replied matter-of-factly.

"How so?"

"I don't know."

"Is it because of the red ribbon?"

"Yeah, I guess."

Terri noticed that the red ribbon was hiding something on the dog's paw. She wondered if Amanda tugged on the ribbon or something. She didn't see anything when she first found the dog in the store, but it had her curious.

"Can I see Violet Red for a second?"

"She's sleeping right now," Amanda responded. "I don't want to wake her up."

"Well, I wouldn't want to disturb her sleeping," Terri said, smiling. Then she remembered hearing her daughter talking to someone in the room. "Who were you talking to earlier?"

"Violet Red, of course," she said as she reached for one of her other toys on the bed. "She was telling me a cute poem."

"Oh? Is that what tired her out?"

"She got sleepy."

"Rhyming sometimes does that to dogs," Teri joked. "Do you remember the poem she told you?"

"I don't think you'd like it."

"I like poems. Go on," Terri urged.

"Two little girls, dressed in red. One girl alive, the other one dead—"

What is this?

Amanda continued. "Don't close your eyes, don't rest your head. For she is watching – the dead girl in red."

Terri shifted uncomfortably on the bed. This little poem was rather disturbing. It wasn't something she imagined Amanda could come up with. She expected something completely different, not this Poe-esque ballad of dead little girls. Amanda wasn't one to come up with scary stuff. She hated scary movies and had nightmares for weeks after letting her read *Scary Stories to Tell in the Dark*. It was that little book that caused her daughter to hate scary stuff. She couldn't blame her – those images were very unforgettable.

"Where did you hear that, honey?" Terri asked, dreading the answer her little girl was about to give her.

Without hesitation, Amanda answered, "Violet Red told me."

-5-

The poem about the two girls haunted Terri for the next couple days. It was the way the poem sounded. It was the way the poem was told to her that invaded her mind, like the way a song on the radio would keep playing in your mind after hearing it several times.

Two little girls dressed in red.

One girl alive, the other one dead.

Don't close your eyes, don't rest your head.

For she is watching – the dead girl in red.

It sent shivers up and down her spine. No matter how hard she tried to drown out the memory, it stuck with her. Delana had suggested that Amanda probably read it in a book at school or something. But Terri was not convinced.

She asked her author/book nerd friend about the poem a day later, and she didn't remember reading it anywhere. Even the book nerd, who loved creepy, macabre shit, found the poem to be disturbing.

Well, her friend said that "a little girl reciting that kind of poem was enough to disturb anyone."

It was bad enough the poem even existed. What made the auditory memory worse was that it was told in her daughter's soft, nearly melancholy tone.

And then the dreams began. She would wake up in a cold

sweat, clutching Delana's arm to calm her nerves. The first night she had a dream of being shoved inside and locked in a closet. It made her dread going to bed at night. Delana suggested taking one of her sleeping pills, but Terri didn't like to medicate just because she was having strange dreams.

Where is this dream even coming from? She thought back at anything she may have heard on the radio, watched on the TV, or read in the papers, but nothing came to mind. They had found that poor homeless guy who was found with his head severed, but that didn't relate in any way to children being locked in a closet.

Consulting a dream dictionary she had purchased a while back when she was into dream interpretation, she wondered if maybe dreaming about closets was in some way related to when she came out, after she had divorced Jeff. Her parents were indifferent about the situation; of course, they protested, saying borderline homophobic things like, "But you married a man!" or her favorite knee-jerk response, "You're just confused – you have a little girl!"

Recollecting those responses from both her parents, and even her gay cousin Rhett, she had to laugh. She couldn't blame them for being surprised. Nobody knew – not even Terri herself!

But the closet could have other interpretations. Her dictionary said that sometimes if you were dreaming about a closet, you were struggling with the way you viewed yourself. It could also potentially mean that you have a lot of things to sort out. It made sense to her. She didn't have a lot of self-confidence and sometimes she thought she looked ugly, no matter how often Delana told her how beautiful she looked in the mornings after waking up.

You couldn't just interpret a dream like this and focus solely on one thing, though. There were other things in the dream that had the potential to change the whole meaning of the dream. She recollected that she felt an adult pushing her inside the closet. Maybe it meant being forced to examine yourself. Or maybe it meant being forced to sort out your life.

And for some reason, her mind shifted to actually cleaning her actual closet. She had a bunch of stuff in there that she never used anymore, several outfits that no longer fit her well. She decided to take at least thirty minutes to sort out the stuff in the closet.

"Hey, Delana!" she shouted from the bedroom. Delana was in the bathroom, putting on her makeup when Terri suddenly decided to clean the closet. "Come here!"

Delana walked in the room, looking stunning in her dark blue outfit and painted face. "What's up?"

"Take a look at this," she said, setting aside a box full of old trinkets. "I haven't seen these in years."

"What is all this stuff?" Delana made herself comfortable on the floor, intrigued with all the stuff in the box.

"It's stuff I thought my Mom gave away when I moved out of the house," Terri replied as she took item by item out of the box. "I could sell these things."

"Not a bad idea, but why did you need me in here to recollect over dusty trinkets?"

"Oh, well I thought you would be interested in this," she answered, holding up a battered box housing a Ouija board.

"No way," Delana whispered, excitement rising in her voice. "You had one of those?"

"When I was fourteen. We played with this on a couple slumber parties in my bedroom."

"My dad threw mine out when I was twelve," Delana remembered. "He was so pissed when he saw me and my friend Jolene messing with the board. He kicked her out and told her to never come around again."

Then, after a brief pause, Delana said, "Sucked too. She was my first kiss."

"You little homo," Terri chuckled, playfully pushing Delana aside. "But then again, that doesn't surprise me."

Delana took the board out of its box, setting the old

board on top of it. "You wanna ask the magic board some questions?"

Terri laughed. "Sure, why not?"

"I'll go first," she said, putting the tips of her fingers lightly on the planchette. Terri followed suit. "Tell me, oh magic board, will we ever win a million dollars?"

No response.

"Oh, come now," Terri scoffed. "We have to ask better questions than that!"

"All right then, Miss Psychic, what do you want to ask the spirits of the deceased?" Delana glanced up at Terri, waiting expectantly.

"Is there anyone in the room with us? How many are there in the room?"

"You're asking too many questions."

"Oh, shut up."

"My God," Delana whispered. "It's actually moving."

"You're pushing it."

"No, I'm not."

"Come on, don't be silly."

"I swear on my mother's grave—"

"Your mom's still alive."

"You're right, she is, and I'm totally fucking with you."

Terri got up from the floor, shaking her head. "You're so lame, Delana," she laughed, heading into the bathroom. Delana continued sorting through the rest of the junk in the closet, her attention completely focused on what other treasures they would find.

She didn't notice the planchette moving to the number three. Terri came back in the room, gathering up the things. "I think I'm gonna throw these all in the box and sell them at the store. There's nothing sentimental in there anyway."

"You sure? I think we should keep the board."

"Nah, I would rather not have Amanda messing around with the board," Terri replied, placing the game back in its box.

"You don't actually believe all that hokey stuff, do you?"

"I don't, no," Terri said, scratching her cheek. "It's all just a mindfuck. But you know how little girls are. Very suggestive."

The poem resumed its rhythm in her mind again.

"But what if I want it?"

"Then hand me $40.00, cuz that's how much I'm selling it for."

"Do you accept kisses as payment?"

"It's leaving this house," Terri said, smirking. "But I do accept kisses."

Delana kissed Terri as she prepared to leave for the store. "Now do I get the board?"

Terri pretended to think about it for a while. She was about to remark with something smart, but the sound of something falling to the ground caught her attention.

She left the room and saw Delana's painting had fallen. Again.

"God damn," Terri said, annoyed. "Can't you just hang that up instead of keeping it on the bookcase? This is the fourth time it's fallen."

"Yeah, I'll hang it up. I don't know why it keeps falling."

Sighing, Terri adjusted the box in her arms. "It was probably too close to the edge or something. It has those little hanging things on it, doesn't it?"

"No, it doesn't. But those are easy to get and install," Delana said as she picked up her painting.

"Problem solved, then," Terri said, taking off for the antique store.

IDA HAD NOT completely come back to the house just yet. She had decided to stay with her cousin and his friend for a few days after she finally left treatment. Jeff understood why – Patrick had just moved to the area, and they had a lot of catching up to do. He never met him before until a few hours ago, when he stopped by to pick up a few things Ida had forgotten.

"How's she doing?" Jeff asked him as he passed a glass of whiskey over his way.

"Adjusting," Patrick replied, frowning. "I mean, it's not bad or anything." Jeff had given him an inquiring look.

"What do you mean, 'adjusting?'"

"Adjusting to me moving into the neighborhood," Patrick smirked, gulping down the alcohol. "We've always been super close – it's been a few years since she's seen me. But she had no idea I lost a lot of weight."

"That's awesome, man."

"Thanks. I thought she was about to assault me when I picked her up from the treatment center. She didn't recognize me at first. Thought I was a rapist or something."

Jeff snorted. "That's kinda funny."

"Yeah. So, I said a couple things she would remember, and she fainted. She actually *fainted.* 'You lost a fuck-ton of weight!' she cried when she finally woke up. So, anyways, she's like super happy for me – but she's totally obsessing over my weight loss. That's what I meant about her adjusting. She's not used to seeing 130 pounds of Patrick."

Jeff supposed it would be a strange adjustment for anyone if they reunited with someone, friend or not, if they had lost a lot of weight. You remember someone who had a completely different look, a different body, and you expect them to look the same way. When they come around for the first time in years, it suddenly dawns on you just how much time can change people.

"Anyways, I should probably get going," Patrick said as he stood up from the couch. "Thanks for the drink."

"Feel free to come around anytime, Pat. It was great to finally meet you," Jeff said, also standing. Looking at the time, he only had about twenty minutes before he had to pick up Amanda from school.

"It was great to meet you too," Patrick said, almost close

to the door. Then he realized why he was there in the first place. "Oh, shit."

Jeff laughed, picking up the couple bags sitting next to him. "Forget something?"

"Ida would kill me if I forgot her things."

"You'd probably be stuck in a wheelchair. She'd break your legs."

"You have experience?"

Jeff grinned. "Let's just say it is one of my few regrets."

AMANDA'S SCHOOL WAS only a few minutes away from Jeff's house. As he stole a glance at the time on the way to her school, he couldn't help but find himself getting excited for the weather to get warmer, so he could walk her to school and back home.

He was there a bit earlier than normal. A few parents were parked in the lot, smoking in their cars as they waited for the right time to make their way inside and pick up their kids. Jeff turned up the radio as he waited for 3:00 to roll around. Leaning his seat back, he closed his eyes, letting the guitar solo overwhelm him.

He wondered how things would be different had he actually followed his dreams instead of marrying young. He didn't particularly love his job, but he did get some satisfaction from what he did for a living. But the long guitar solo in the song brought him back to when he was seventeen years old. At that age, he felt his talents were well-suited for working in real estate. He knew he had a great mind for business, but as fate would have it, Jeff's great cooking surpassed his knack for numbers and managing people.

Instead, he was lead chef at a local Italian restaurant. His ability to make sensational sauces and knowing how to make his own pasta won over the owner. He had the job for the past seven years, and even though he still thought about going back to school and getting an MBA, the idea of leaving the business no longer appealed to him like it did before.

Then again, he did not have to restrict himself to real estate. The MBA would also be great for starting up his own restaurant and having even more freedom to do as he pleased. He did have freedom to do what he wanted to the recipes and was basically the sole person responsible for the daily special but owning a restaurant would grant him things he had never even dreamed of before.

Jeff adjusted himself and looked at the time. He got out of his car and locked the doors, making his way inside the school, toward Amanda's classroom. As he stepped in the room, he saw Amanda at her little desk, the dog Terri gave her for Christmas sitting on the corner. Her teacher, Miss Ginger Hammett, was standing next to her, talking to her about something and setting a piece of paper down. As he got closer, he heard a bit of the exchange.

"…need to focus more on these longer words. You have the general idea on how the words sound, though."

"Yes, Miss Hammett," Amanda replied, her head lowered in embarrassment. Jeff knew that look very well.

Miss Hammett noticed Jeff walking over to the desk. He wondered if she ever smiled. Her eyes barely even gave a hint of satisfaction, making Jeff wonder if she really did want to become a teacher. Maybe she had similar dreams to Jeff? Who knew?

She cleared her throat. "Mr. Toms. How are you doing today?"

"Just fine, thanks," he responded. "Is there something I need to be aware of?"

"Amanda seems to be performing below my expectations, and the school's, for what I expect from the other students. She really needs help with the longer words. I was just telling her that she is able to pronounce the words just fine, but the spelling isn't quite to my standards."

"Is this something we can take home tonight and look over?" asked Jeff.

Miss Hammett glanced at the paper again. "Yes, I just graded these earlier today."

"Great," he said, taking the paper from the desk and looking it over. He remembered well the red markings on the paper – it always made him nervous to bring his homework home for his parents to review. Not that they cared much, but they did what they could to help him with his math, in particular.

"How is she doing in math?"

"I'd like you to stop abbreviating words when you're around your daughter, Mr. Toms. The correct wordage for that sentence is, 'How is she *performing* in *mathematics*. Not 'doing;' not 'math.' It's one of the spelling words, as you would have seen if you looked at the spelling test," she said curtly. Jeff had to restrain himself from saying something smart to her.

"Right, of course. We will work on these words tonight."

"It is greatly appreciated, Mr. Toms."

"You did not answer my question, Miss Hammett. How is she performing in mathematics?" he asked, putting an exaggerated emphasis on the words she used just a second ago.

Miss Hammett narrowed her eyes, picking up Jeff's cynicism. "That's another thing she needs to really focus on, Mr. Toms. By now, I expect all my students to be able to add triple-digit numbers without consulting a calculator. Please take the time to review this as well," she said sternly, handing off another sheet of paper marked with a lot of red.

"Certainly. Thank you, Miss Hammett," Jeff said, picking up Amanda's bag and placing the papers in her book-filled bag.

"Oh, and one more thing," Miss Hammett said before they left the classroom. "I told your daughter that all toys must be placed in her bag during study hours. I don't mind having the toys on display when they're taking breaks from their work, but it's very inappropriate to have them on display when they should be paying attention in class. Amanda, on at least two occasions today, deliberately neglected to put her stuffed animal in her bag."

"Her name is Violet Red," Amanda snapped.

Jeff was stunned. Amanda had so much respect for her teachers. The fact she spoke back to her teacher was surprising. "Amanda! You apologize to Miss Hammett, now!"

Amanda looked at her dad, then back to Miss Hammett. "I'm sorry," she murmured.

"Please speak up louder so I can hear you clearly, Amanda," she requested.

"I said that I was sorry, okay?" Amanda retorted, grabbing her bag. Before Jeff could stop her, she had left the room to throw on her winter coat. Jeff quickly looked over at Miss Hammett and mouthed an apology for her behavior. Her lips were pressed so tightly against each other as she coldly walked away and went back to her large desk.

"I don't know what is going on with her," she finally said after situating herself, opening up one of the many notebooks scattered on the desk, "but this is unacceptable behavior. I'm going to talk to her guidance counselor and see if she can see her at some point tomorrow."

Jeff couldn't help but agree with her. "That's fine by me."

"If she does this again," Miss Hammett said, looking up at Jeff, "and I hope she doesn't repeat this behavior, I will have to request for in-school suspension."

Jeff stared at her. "In-school suspension? You can't be serious."

"I am, Mr. Toms," she said briskly.

"Over the whole math—I mean, mathematics and spelling stuff? Over her brief attitude? That seems very extreme to me."

"If you were here for the entire time school is in session, you would understand why I would suggest in-school suspension. These kids need an attitude adjustment, and they're learning bad behavior somewhere. You need to squash it before it turns into anything worse. Do you, or do you not, agree with me?"

Jeff had enough, but he didn't really feel like exploding in front of her. He knew she had to face a lot of challenges with a fair number of outbursts and could slightly understand where she might be coming from. But this was Amanda. She's just like one of her stuffed toys – sweet and kind. Amanda wouldn't turn into one of those bad kids overnight.

"I don't think you really know what you're talking about, Miss Hammett, but I'll definitely be having a talk with her when we get home. Have a good night."

THE MOMENT THEY left the school and got into the car, Amanda pulled out the stuffed dog from her bag and placed it on her lap like it was a real dog. She petted the little pup and started whispering to it. Jeff could hear a bit of what she was saying but couldn't quite hear exactly what she was saying. As he began driving, he could hear her a bit more clearly. She was telling the dog how good he was, and how happy she was to have the dog. It seemed very odd to him, but he remained silent until they walked inside.

Amanda was about to head into her room when Jeff stopped her, disappointedly looking at her. "Halt there, little missy," he said, pursing his chapped lips.

Jesus, I need to get a thing of chap stick, he thought to himself. *Get back on track, you need to talk to your daughter.*

Amanda looked up at her dad. She could sense he was upset with her, and it made her clutch her stuffed animal tighter than she ever had before.

She could swear she heard someone near her cry out in pain.

"We need to talk about your behavior at school. Can you set down Violet Rose for me, please?"

"It's Violet Red, daddy," she corrected him.

"I don't care about the toy right now," he snapped back at her, the same way she had just done to him. "Listen to me!"

Amanda was silent. He never raised his voice at her, and it scared her. Jeff could see how his outburst affected her, but for some reason he didn't care. He wanted to frighten her a bit, so that she could do better.

"Your teacher told you several times not to be playing with your toys when she's in front of the chalkboard. I want to know why you disobeyed your teacher."

Amanda was quiet. She was trying to find the words to say but was struggling. Jeff could tell – she always sniffled when she was cornered and had a hard time speaking. She looked at the dog, then looked back at her daddy. "She wouldn't let me, Daddy," she whispered.

"Who wouldn't let you? One of the kids sitting next to you?"

"No. Violet Red told me."

"You're lying to me."

"Daddy, I'm not lying. Violet Red—"

"Toys don't talk back to children, Amanda. Don't be silly. I'm going to ask you again – why did you disobey Miss Hammett?"

"Because she doesn't like being stuck in my bag for a long time."

"That's not a reason," Jeff snapped. "Amanda, I think your toy needs to stay at home when you're at school. No more toys, okay?"

"Violet Red doesn't want to stay at home. She gets lonely."

Jeff paused himself from freaking out at her. He had the sudden urge to tell her off, to tell her that a toy can't get lonely, that a toy does not experience human emotions. He wanted to tell her that toys stay at home, and don't go to school with them. But he suddenly remembered that this was a child in front of him, that yelling at her would only make her rebel – after all, he had moments when he was her age when all he wanted to do was disobey his teachers.

Jeff sat down next to her, briefly acknowledging the stuffed animal she again had placed in her lap. As he considered the words he was going to say to her, memories of Lil Pup came back to him. He swallowed nervously before he began to speak. It was Terri who was great with disciplining Amanda when it was needed. He never had the opportunity to do so, until now. "You know, when I was your age, I had a little chihuahua dog. My parents got him when I was your age. I loved my little buddy. When I would come home from school, Lil Pup would always bark and come running over to me. I'd pick him up and I'd hug him. And I wanted nothing more but to bring him to school with me and show him off to everyone, I guess, because I wanted to make them jealous."

"What does 'jealous' mean?" Amanda interrupted.

"It means that you have something that you want people to wish they had," Jeff answered. "But you want to know what my mom told me when I tried to slip him in my school bag?"

"What?"

"She told me that Lil Pup wasn't meant to be at school. That he had to stay at home and be a good dog. 'School wasn't meant for dogs, and dogs weren't meant for school,' she told me. I was mad at my mom for not letting me take the dog to school, but I put him back on the ground and let him run around the room.

"I know you love Violet Ro—I mean, Violet Red, but she's meant to be at home. She needs to be around others like her." Jeff smiled. He liked where he was going with this. "I bet, when you're not home, they all get together for tea and cookies, and laugh and talk and do what normal stuffed animals do when you're not with them. What do you think they do when you're at school?"

Amanda smiled. She loved the idea of her toys sitting at

her little green table, laughing and eating cookies. "I guess they do," she responded. "What kind of cookies do you think they like?"

"Umm," Jeff pretended to think. "I bet they like chocolate walnut cookies!"

Amanda made a face. "You're silly, Daddy. Nobody likes walnuts in their cookies!"

"Well then I guess I'm a Nobody," Jeff teased.

"Can we have cookies for supper?"

The door suddenly opened, revealing Ida. Jeff looked at her. Her brother was right – she was looking much better than she did before going into treatment.

"Ida?" Jeff asked, surprised at her appearance.

"Hey," she said, smiling. She looked at Amanda, her eyes glistening as she took a seat on the couch with her. Amanda moved over to the far corner of the couch.

"Amanda, I'm hurt," she said, frowning.

Jeff glanced at his wife, floored by her attitude. Maybe she has changed, for the better!

"You hurt me," Amanda replied, barely audible.

Ida looked at Jeff, disappointment burning inside her eyes. "Hey kiddo, can you look at me for a second, please?"

It took Amanda all her willpower to obey, but she relented and looked at her. She had a hard time looking at the woman who verbally assaulted her. She could still hear Ida saying those horrible things to her before she went to the hospital.

"I'm sorry for saying really mean things to you," Ida began, sounding very much apologetic. "You aren't all those things I said. You're a sweet little girl, and I think you're a gift from Heaven."

Jeff had to wonder if he was in some sort of strange alien fantasy flick. She hated children, and Amanda was no exception to the rule, but the things she was saying he actually believed. He couldn't help but think she was also directing the words to him as well, in her own way.

"Are you really sorry for hurting me?" Amanda asked, her voice small and apprehensive.

"I am. I really am," answered Ida. She ushered Amanda over to her and hugged her. Amanda could feel tears welling up inside of her.

There was a moment of silence as the two girls held each other on the couch, with Violet Red sitting on the couch, threatening to fall down to the floor.

And if anyone in the room listened very closely, they would have heard a small, child-like voice try to tell Amanda that Ida wasn't sorry.

She wasn't sorry at all.

AFTER DINNER, JEFF had Amanda get her school bag from her room, so they could review spelling and her math. Jeff looked again at the marked-up assignment, the red glaring at him as though he was the one who fucked everything up.

Mathematics.

Incredible.

Apprehensive.

Those were just a couple words marked in red. Miss Hammett was on to something – she was able to understand how the words sounded, but she spelled them the way she thought they were spelled.

Mathumetics.

Incrudable.

Aprehinsif.

He wondered what the best way he could get her to understand how to spell the words. He had the sudden wish that he was dating an English teacher but laughed at himself. No strong-minded teacher would want to date him! He remembered how badly he had struggled with spelling when he was in third grade.

But even more than that, he hated how his dad would

react when he came home with a red-marked assignment.

Jeff also took a look at the math assignment. For a moment, he thought that it was expecting a lot from these kids to be perfectly able to get these math problems right. Then again, he was no math whiz, either. He had no idea what was expected of third graders nowadays.

What was Miss Hammett expecting, these kids to become engineers or architects?

Jeff scratched his head. The first few problems were simple. 200+450 was one of the problems Amanda was able to do just fine.

650.

He looked at the next problem. 211+122. He could clearly see that the answer was 333, but Amanda had written down 311. Not quite sure how she got that number from that problem, but that was something he would help her with.

The next problem was also perplexing.

625+511.

Amanda had written down 800.

He attempted to visualize Amanda's method of thinking. He knew the answer was over 1000. But for some reason Amanda wasn't able to grasp numbers past 1000.

Maybe she had a learning disability, and he wasn't aware of it? Jeff wasn't sure, but he didn't want to jump the gun to get Amanda tested. He had a small inkling she probably had ADD.

The idea of getting her tested became even more prominent as he attempted to help Amanda with the assignments. Something wasn't clicking with her, and she was distracted by the cookies on the table. He got up from the table and placed the plate on the counter behind him.

"Gotta focus, kiddo," he said encouragingly.

"I'm trying. Really," Amanda urged.

"Want to let me try?" Ida asked as she walked into the room, helping herself to another cookie. Chewing, she sat down in the chair next to Amanda. "What do we have here?"

"We have 452 plus 60."

"Ok," Ida said, furrowing her brow. "I think I know what to do."

Looking at Amanda, Ida stole a piece of scrap paper lying on the table. She wrote down something and handed it to Amanda.

45+6

"That's easy," Amanda replied, smiling. "Six is just five with an extra one."

"Yep, that's right," Ida said, nodding her head.

"So, that would be 51, right?"

Jeff grinned. "You got it!" He reached out his hand for Amanda to clap, and she obliged.

"Now, what do you get when you add nothing to two?" Ida continued.

"Two, of course," Amanda replied back.

"Now, let's squish these two numbers together," Ida said, finishing the cookie. "We're not adding them together but squishing them. What is 51 squished next to the number 2?"

"512," Amanda said self-assuredly.

"See how easy that is?" Ida asked.

"Yeah!" Amanda exclaimed.

"Well, I think I've been outsmarted," Jeff said, standing up. "You wanna take over from here?"

"Why not? This is kinda fun!" Ida said.

Yup. Aliens had invaded her body.

Within just five minutes, Amanda was finally understanding the assignment. Ida noticed that the stuffed dog was sitting on the table, and for some reason she felt nervous. Something was very peculiar about the toy, but she couldn't put a finger on what it was. "Can I see your toy?" she asked Amanda.

Amanda nodded her head. She was starting to feel very comfortable around Ida. The way Ida was helping her and treating her felt really good to her.

She took the stuffed animal from its place on the table,

studying it carefully. The red ribbon caught her attention. She tugged at it.

It felt as though someone had shoved a pin in her thumb and index finger. She exclaimed and tossed the toy to the floor.

Amanda looked at Ida reproachfully. "You hurt Violet Red," she whispered.

"It's a fucking toy!" yelled Ida. Jeff came running into the room.

"What's going on?" he demanded, looking straight at Ida.

Now things were getting back to normal.

"That stupid toy. I think there's a needle in there, but I didn't see anything sticking out," she said quickly.

Jeff picked up the dog from the floor. He looked the toy over, looking at the red ribbon on the paw. There wasn't anything sticking out from the ribbon. He wondered if something was under the ribbon, something sticking out, but it would have stuck out.

"I don't see anything, either," Jeff replied.

"Maybe I was just shocked or something, a nerve, maybe?" Ida suggested.

"Maybe," Jeff said. "Amanda, can you go to your room while I talk to Ida for a second? You can take another cookie, if you want."

Amanda went away from the room, taking a cookie with her.

"Next time you scream at her, make sure your fucking bags are packed, because you'll be out of this house within a blink of a fucking eye, d'you hear me?" he hissed at her.

-6-

A stuffed animal couldn't do much harm.

It was just a stuffed animal.

Ida continued to obsess over Amanda's toy. She kept thinking over and over that there had to have been a needle. The pain that came over her fingers was no pinched nerve. It couldn't have been. She had experienced the pain of a pinched nerve.

No, it felt like something stabbed her.

She wanted desperately to look that animal over, but Amanda was fast asleep in bed after what happened in the kitchen. Violet Red was tucked in bed with her. She walked past Amanda's room, stopping at the door, pondering whether or not to open the door and examine the toy closely.

And she did.

She crept in her room. Her small night light was plugged in, so she was able to see the kid's room.

Damn it.

She had the stuffed animal tucked in bed with her. She edged closer to the bed, keeping an eye on Amanda, so as not to awaken her. There had to have been something inside that red ribbon tied to the paw of that dog. As she neared closer to the bed, an uneasy feeling came over her, like when you drink cold water on an empty stomach. The coldness crept inside her stomach as she got even closer, seeing the dog halfway under the covers.

Great, I can take it from the covers and take a closer look. There's no way Amanda will know.

She lightly took the dog by its head and slowly removed it from the heavy blanket over Jeff's daughter.

She does look really cute when she's sleeping, that little witch.

Bringing it over to the night light, she looked the toy over again, feeling the soft material of the toy. A soft noise came from Amanda's bed. She was stirring, but not awakening.

Maybe if I grab that little tweezers on her dresser, I can see what's under it.

She heard Jeff walking down the hall as she was about to take the tweezers and pinch the ribbon. The door slowly opened. Jeff stood outside of the room, looking inside. He saw what Ida was doing.

"Get out of there," he whispered.

Annoyed, Ida placed the tweezers back where they belonged, put the toy next to it, and walked out of the room.

"What were you doing?"

"Nothing," Ida said quickly.

"Didn't look like nothing to me."

Ida dropped her arms to the side. "Okay, I wanted to take a look at that stuffed animal. Is that a crime?"

"You snuck into my daughter's room, Ida. That's just… It's weird. You couldn't wait until morning?"

"Sorry, I know I shouldn't have, but my curiosity got the better of me."

Jeff looked at Ida inquisitively, wondering if she was really telling the truth, but he did see tweezers in her hand, and she *was* about to do something to that toy. He was wondering if that toy was really safe, too. "I'm curious too, to be honest."

Ida let out a breath of relief. "You're right. It can wait until later."

"Let's go to bed. I'm exhausted," Jeff yawned, making his way into the bedroom.

"I am too," Ida replied. "I'm gonna take a shower."

"Make it quick," Jeff winked.

Ida smirked. "You could always… you know."

"Nah, you go shower. I can wait. Think about that hot water all over your naked body."

She laughed. "Keep yourself busy. Five minutes."

"Only five minutes?" Jeff whined playfully.

Ida smirked as she touched the bottom of his small chin, kissed him on the nose, and left to the bathroom, stripping off her clothes. She turned on the water and stepped inside. Immediately, she released another held breath, grateful for the shower. The water pressure at the rehab center was something to be desired – it was so terrible she felt dirty after showering. And it didn't help matters that it was a community shower, with other naked women, shampooing their breasts and talking about their day and how happy they were that they were making progress.

There was one woman there that caught her attention. She was a short, chubby woman who resented being there and demanded that her food was delivered to her room. She wanted no contact with anyone and always had to be dragged out of her room for her group and individual therapy sessions. Ida immediately took a liking to her, and they hit it off rather well. She had two adult children who continued to impress on her what her drinking was doing to her grandchildren.

She didn't care. She drank – like most of them did – to escape their problems. It was escapism for them. Instead of reaching for a book or watching a movie, this woman would pour herself a really large glass of whiskey, maybe add a little bit of soda, and down it within five minutes.

Then she'd make another. And another.

Until finally she was so incoherent she would pass out and not wake up until two in the afternoon.

Ida wasn't like that. She liked to savor her drinks, but she admitted in group therapy that she wanted the feeling of being drunk to take its due course. She wanted it to sink in.

But after maybe two large glasses, she stopped savoring and started acting like a sorority sister. The woman who caught her attention laughed at her when she told the group about how she drank, and Ida came really close to having an altercation with this woman. She didn't, though. Ida could understand why this woman did what she did, and to her surprise, ended up feeling really sorry for her. The more she heard the old woman's story, the more she shared with the group, the more Ida realized she did not want to end up like this bitter, old woman.

She killed herself after three days of treatment.

The nurses had to escort Ida out of the room – she was clinging to the woman's bedside, sobbing and sobbing, repeating the same thing over and over again: "I don't want this to be me. I don't want to die. I don't want this to be me."

That was when she realized she needed to stop drinking altogether.

But something about that damned stuffed dog gave her the sudden desire to reach into Jeff's cabinet and pour herself a drink. She couldn't stop thinking about the dog, couldn't stop thinking about what was underneath that stupid, red ribbon. Those blue eyes staring at you accusingly for wanting to see what was underneath the ribbon.

Ida began scrubbing her body with Jeff's bar soap when she heard it. It sounded like someone was on the radio, singing something, but with no background music.

It got closer to the shower.

Then she heard it, clear as day. Fear gripped her. The sound of the singing was haunting, enticing.

She stopped the water, and as though the faucet was a radio knob, the singing stopped. But she still felt uneasy, as though someone was behind the shower curtain.

She saw nothing.

Relieved, she grabbed the towel from the rack and began to dry herself off, looking at herself in the mirror.

You're losing it, girl.

She looked down at the counter and noticed that her face wash was missing.

I know I put it back in the bathroom when I came back here.

Perturbed, she began to search the floor of the bathroom, looking to see where her face wash may have fallen.

Then it started again. That singing. That strange voice.

Coming from nowhere.

Two little girls, dressed in red

One girl alive, the other one dead.

Don't close your eyes, don't rest your head.

She is watching - the dead girl in red.

Ida screamed, hitting her head hard on the bathroom sink. The words, "the dead girl in red," continued repeating in her head until everything around her went black.

"SHE'LL BE OKAY, right?" was the first thing she heard when she finally woke up.

She didn't open her eyes, but she heard someone speaking to Jeff. The sound of the stranger's voice was enough for her to open her eyes, but she wasn't able to see very clearly. She could sense she wasn't home.

"Just a mild concussion," the other voice said. "We'll have to watch her for a bit, make sure there wasn't any significant damage."

"For how long?"

"A twenty-four-hour visit, to be exact," the doctor responded.

Twenty-four hours?

Ida groaned.

"You're awake," Jeff whispered. "What happened?"

Ida took a breath and attempted to recollect what she could. The doctor made some noises.

"Might need to keep her longer," the doctor mused. "Auditory hallucinations are a sign of something that may already have been present prior to her accident."

"Keep her for as long as you need, doc," Jeff said, sounding very grim.

"No," Ida murmured. "I don't want to stay here."

"It won't be for very long, Mrs. Toms," the doctor responded. "We need to treat this very seriously. Have you heard voices like this before?"

"No," Ida grumbled. "No, I haven't."

"I see," the doctor pursed his lips. "We'll have to order some more tests. Bring in a psychiatrist."

"A psychiatrist? No, doc. I'm not crazy," Ida replied scornfully. "I'm not crazy."

"No, you're not crazy. What you experienced lately is very traumatic. We need to—"

She started screaming. "No! Fuck you guys!" She tried to tear off the things attached to her arm but was unsuccessful. The doctor called for help and two nurses came barging in.

"Ida, please," Jeff urged her. "Please."

But she wouldn't let up. She couldn't really sense much, but she felt a needle being pressed against her skin, making her cry out again.

"It's a mild sedative, Mrs. Toms," the doctor explained. "Just a mild sedative."

Ida felt very tired as the medicine hit her system. Jeff looked over at the doctor despairingly, frowning. "Thank you," he said to the doctor.

The doctor frowned. "We'll do what we can. And before you know it, she'll be back home with you."

Jeff looked nervously at his wife. "Do what you can. I'll be here for her." He took Ida's hand in his and squeezed it. "It will be okay. Everything will be okay."

But Ida wasn't too sure about that. Something was there in that bathroom with her, and she knew it wasn't Jeff. It wasn't even Amanda. Something was in that bathroom with her, and it wanted her dead.

-7-

She woke up crying.

Ida looked around her and let out a huge sigh of relief. She was finally out of the hospital! Smiling, she laid down on the comfortable bed and closed her eyes. It was all a dream. She never was in the hospital. She never hit her head. She was back at home. Ida looked over at her right side, expecting to see her husband lying next to her, his chest slowly rising and descending. But he wasn't there with her.

She had no idea why she was crying. She was happy – she had made a huge life change, and everything was the way it should be. Ida attempted to raise a hand to wipe her eyes, but she had a difficult time trying to get her hand to move.

Her wrists felt like she was tied up in bed. She wasn't able to move. The feeling that she was being watched came over her, and she darted her eyes in the dark room, trying to find whoever was watching her in the darkness.

But there wasn't anybody there.

The sound of a radio playing caught her attention. She strained to hear what was being sung, or what was being said. It sounded really tinny, the sound of the radio coming from somewhere other than the bedroom.

The voice on the radio grew louder, and she could finally make out the words being sung. Fear gripped her. The song was familiar. It was one she heard recently.

Two little girls dressed in red.

One girl alive, the other one dead.

Don't close your eyes, don't rest your head.

She is watching – the dead girl in red.

The door to the bedroom opened, but nobody was there. It was like the wind blew it open. Even though there was nobody there to open the door and creep inside, she knew there was something standing in the doorway, watching her.

Waiting for her.

She attempted to close her eyes, but she could not will her eye lids to shut down. The feeling of walking into a walk-in freezer washed over her. Whatever invisible entity had broken the sanctity of the room was now so close to her, she could smell it. It smelled of dead flowers and dirt. She could even hear something breathing right next to her.

The song started up again.

"No, please," Ida cried. "Leave me alone. Please, leave me alone!"

IDA WOKE UP screaming. The other patient in the hospital room turned her head to stare at her. She snapped her head over to give the woman an accusatory look, feeling eyes glued on her.

"What are you staring at?" she cried.

"You were talking in your sleep, then you woke up," the woman said. "I didn't mean to startle you."

"Mind your own business," Ida hissed. "I had a nightmare. That's all."

"Must've been some nightmare," the woman said. "I almost called the nurses into the room."

"Don't talk to me!" yelled Ida. She had no idea who this woman was, but she needed to learn to mind herself. She didn't care what this woman was in the hospital for and went back to close her eyes. At the same time, she was too scared to fall asleep. She didn't want the dream to come back, but she was hoping and praying for peaceful dreams.

"Is it okay if I sing to you?" the woman asked her.

"I don't want to hear your voice. I don't want to hear you talking. I don't want to hear you sing. Leave. Me. Alone!" Ida yelled. She was tempted to grab the remote and call for the nurse.

The woman acted as though she didn't hear a word Ida said, and broke out in song:

"Two little girls dressed in red.
One girl alive, the other one dead.
Don't close your eyes, don't rest your head.
For she is watching – the dead girl in red."

Ida froze. Out of the corner of her eye, she could see the bed-ridden woman get up from the bed and slowly approach her.

"This isn't possible," Ida whispered, fear overwhelming her. She wanted to get up and run out of that room, but she saw the door was closed and she was still rather weak. "This isn't possible."

The woman who was just a few inches taller than her was shrinking down in size, transforming into a little black girl that seemed to be about Amanda's age. A red ribbon was tied to her wrist. It was glowing so brightly Ida couldn't stand it anymore.

Ida closed her eyes. Maybe this was another nightmare brought on by the medication. She heard that some people had horrific dreams while sedated.

Yes, that's what this is. It's nothing more than a drug-induced nightmare.

Or is it a night terror? Ida could never really tell the difference between the two.

She opened her eyes, and the woman was gone. She let out a sigh of relief as she reached for the glass next to her. Some water would definitely do her good. She needed the refreshing, cool water on her tongue.

As she grabbed the glass, it crashed to the floor.

"Damn it," she whispered.

Something grabbed her neck and squeezed. Ida choked. She couldn't see her assailant. Something was choking the life out of her, and she couldn't see who it was.

She could feel herself growing light as a feather. Her sight was getting hazy, and the sensation of walking on clouds took her over.

It wasn't a nightmare this time. This time, it was real.

DOING ROUNDS ON the night shift was probably one of the things Bertha liked the most about her job. Sometimes, the patients would still be awake, and she would chat with them for at least a minute or two before moving onto the next room. Her supervisor reprimanded her a couple times for doing so, but the others enjoyed how much Bertha cared for the patients. The other nurses didn't seem to mind. Bertha was one-of-a-kind. In the words of one of the patients who had to stay about two days, "Bertha's an angel. Don't you fucking fire her for doing what y'all should be doing."

She approached room 416 and pushed the door open. It was strange to her that the door was closed. Doors weren't supposed to be closed on this wing. She walked in the room and looked around. Something felt very off about the room. Hesitating, she walked deeper into the room, tempted to turn the light on. She decided against it as she drew nearer to one of the beds.

Something wet was on the floor. She took the flashlight out and turned it on.

There was a dark puddle of blood on the floor. Dropping the flashlight, she covered her mouth, but it was of no use – Bertha's scream jolted the other patient awake.

"I'm trying to sleep," the woman hissed at her.

Bertha ignored the woman and called for help. One of the nurses came over to her side and swore.

"My God," Jewel whispered, looking at the dead body on the bed. "What happened?"

Bertha couldn't find the words to answer her coworker. She braved the steps over to the deceased woman and found a deep cut mark on her throat. She explained what she saw to Jewel, being careful to not make contact with the poor woman's blood.

"Suicide?" Jewel asked.

"I don't think so," Bertha said, whispering. "There's no knife in hand, and I don't see anything else that fell to the floor."

"That woman's dead?" the patient next to Ida asked, bewildered.

For a second, the two nurses thought maybe the other woman had done it, but that also proved to not make sense. Bertha noticed a personal walker was next to the other patient's bed. There's no way she could have killed this woman.

"We'll have to phone the police," Jewel said, still looking at Ida's corpse, noting the peculiar look on Ida's face. It looked like she was mid-scream when it happened.

More proof that this woman didn't kill herself. Bertha left the room and picked up the phone to call the police. Something was amiss.

The detectives who arrived at the hospital came to the same agreement as Bertha and Jewel. The woman was murdered; that was a fact. Detective Ian McBride looked over at his partner, Detective Mickey Adams, as he walked back into the hospital room.

"Find anything?" Ian asked his partner.

"Nada. Everyone on this floor swears they saw nobody come in," replied Mickey. "And we're one hundred percent certain her bed-neighbor didn't do this?"

"Very certain," Ian responded.

"But where's the weapon?"

"A good question. There's nothing in this room, aside

from this red ribbon thing next to her pillow. Nothing under the beds. The killer must have taken it with him."

"That's assuming the killer is a male," Mickey said, his eyes on the dead woman. Once again, he looked at the dead body. The cut on the neck looked to be about eight inches across. Red marks covered the neck. "These hand marks are small. Almost like a child's."

"A child couldn't do this."

"No shit," Mickey responded, his face looking grim and concerned. "Here's what I think. The killer chokes her out first, to make sure she's out like a light. Then he grabs a knife and carefully slashes her. That slit is meticulous. Someone wanted to make her suffer."

"But who could it have been?"

Mickey scratched his peach fuzz. "It's the hand marks. It couldn't have been a grown adult."

"And it's definitely not self-inflicted, either."

"This makes no sense to me."

"She has an enemy. This MO is way too personal for it to be a random murder."

Ian turned to one of the nurses who was still in the room. "Any family?"

"She has a husband. I'll get you his contact information," the nurse replied before leaving the room.

Ian turned to Mickey. "You thinking what I'm thinking?"

"What makes you think it was the husband? I keep looking at those handprints. It couldn't have been an adult male."

"Well, once we talk to the widower, I think we'll have some more answers," Ian said as the nurse came back into the room and handed him Jeff's contact information. He read the paper out loud before handing it to Adams.

"You want to know what I really don't like about this job?" Mickey said, pocketing the contact information.

"What's that?"

"It's notifying family about deceased family members,"

Mickey said, not looking forward to making the house call and wishing he was elsewhere. He hated hospitals.

"Fifty bucks says he already knows."

-8-

There was a little girl in Terri's house she hardly recognized anymore. She had the same eyes, the same chin structure as Terri, and – as rare it is now – the same smile that brought with it the cutest dimples ever seen on a little girl's face. The girl who was now visiting every other weekend had the same physical features but did not have the same spirit.

The first thing she thought when she first noticed her daughter acting peculiar was that Ida was back to abusing her daughter. Terri kept going back and forth regarding whether or not she should confront Jeff about it, but the more she considered saying anything, she ended up deciding against it. She watched Amanda sit on the floor of the living room with a cartoon playing on the TV, but the girl who used to be so invested in *The Little Mermaid* was now treating the show like background noise. She was now holding onto the stuffed dog and talking to it, as though it was talking back.

At first, it was cute watching Amanda play with the toy. She and Violet Red were like glue, stuck together and hard to pull away from. Terri actually found it entertaining when she would bring the dog to the dinner table and pretend it was enjoying macaroni and cheese along with everyone else. Even

Delana found it absolutely adorable. As long as Amanda didn't actually "feed" the toy, neither of them found any issue with having Amanda bring the toy to the table with them.

In the beginning, Amanda would take about three members of the Stuffingtons to join Violet Red as they played Tea Party or some kind of classroom game. The stuffed animals would be in a little circle, close together. Delana was the first to notice that as the weeks went along, Amanda would put more of a distance in-between the toys.

"Say, how come Violet Red is so far away from Octo and Meow Stuffingtons today?" asked Delana as she was sitting on the couch one day, reading one of her magazines.

"They're talking to each other," Amanda replied, "brushing" the stuffed dog's hair.

"Oh? What are they talking about?"

"They're just talking."

"Can't you hear what they're saying?" pursued Delana. For some reason, she was getting really curious and invested in the lives of Amanda's toys.

"I suppose," the little girl murmured as she finished with the brush, using her hand to push back the fur on Violet Red. She looked over at the four toys sitting on the floor, then looked back at Delana. "They're talking about me."

"Well, I'm sure they have really nice things to say about you."

"They don't," Amanda replied tonelessly. "That's why they are sitting over there instead of with me."

"Well, that's not very nice." Delana got up from her spot on the couch, sitting in front of Amanda. "Do you want me to have a pep talk with them?"

Amanda looked up at Delana. Delana almost fell back – the look in Amanda's eyes was off. "I suppose. But they won't listen to *you.*"

Delana swallowed hard. "Can I try?"

"Whatever, I guess," Amanda replied in the same tone she had spoken in earlier and went back to coddling her stuffed animal.

Delana didn't think much about what she was about to do, as silly as it was about to look, but she would have done anything to put a smile on the little girl's face. She crawled over to the toys, and in her silliest voice she could muster, said to them, "So, what do you guys have to say for yourselves? Why are you being unkind to your mother?"

It would be ridiculous to expect an answer from the inanimate objects before her, but there she was, on the floor and staring at toys. In a low voice, she changed her voice and replied back, "Because she likes Violet Red more than us."

"Now, Octo Stuffingtons, she loves you just as much as she loves—"

Delana was shocked to see Amanda stomp over to the toys on the floor and grab them as fiercely as she did. "That's not what they're saying! Don't talk to them! You're stupid!"

Delana knew she had a right to stand up and scold Amanda, but she couldn't get herself off the floor. She was too stunned at Amanda's reaction. Her mouth dropped.

The voice that came out wasn't Delana's, but it was Amanda directing her voice to the stuffed animals when she said, "Go to your room, now!"

Delana got herself up from the floor and straightened herself up. "You better go to your room, too. You don't talk to me like that, ever again. Is that clear?"

Amanda smiled, but it wasn't a kind one she was aiming at her mother. "Violet Red says you're stupid, too. And I don't have to listen to you. You're not even a *real mother*."

The words stabbed Delana in the heart. She did her best to not collapse on the couch. "Go to your room, now," she said curtly.

"What's going on here?" Terri asked as she walked into the room, a large box in her arms. "Amanda?"

Before Amanda could say anything to Terri, Delana spoke up. "I don't know what has gotten into her, but she is getting smart with me."

"Amanda, you apologize to Delana, right now," Terri said, shocked that her daughter would be so mean to Delana.

"I'm sorry that you're not a real mother," Amanda smirked as she walked away.

"Hey!" Terri shouted, setting the box down on the couch, then chasing after her daughter. She opened the door and was startled by what she was seeing. There was stuffing all over the floor, decapitated and former stuffed flamingoes, and a pair of large scissors in Amanda's hands. She raised her hand to her mouth, covering it. "What the…"

Amanda saw the look on her mother's face as she grinned, cutting into Octo Stuffingtons' tentacles. Terri grabbed the scissors from her daughter's hands. "We don't cut our toys. And we don't say rude things to adults," Terri said sharply.

But Amanda didn't seem to care. "They were mean to me. And to Violet Red. They deserve what they got."

AS MUCH AS she did not want to, Terri needed to meet with Jeff. Something was grossly amiss, and she needed to figure out what kind of behavior their daughter was exhibiting at Jeff's home. The past few days, she was hoping what she witnessed was just a strange dream. A dream possibly induced by something she had eaten or saw on TV. But no. The reality was that Amanda was not the girl she knew.

She sat at the restaurant, sipping on a tall glass of water, waiting on an order of appetizers she ordered a few moments ago. The restaurant was beautiful and subdued. There was just enough light hitting in just the right places to evoke a feeling of romance, but it wasn't strong enough to make it blatantly obvious. The menu was even more extensive since the last time she had been in. She had a feeling Jeff was partly responsible for at least half of what was now offered.

"At first, he thought I was insane for adding a few more

salads, but as you can see, I won that argument," Jeff said as he took a seat directly across from her.

"I have to admit, that feta raspberry salad sounds really good right now," Terri replied, now glossing over the small wine list.

"You could add shrimp for $3.00 more."

"Please," Terri grinned, finally looking at Jeff. "I just ordered appetizers."

"And your lunch is on my tab," Jeff laughed. "Order it."

Shaking her head, Terri couldn't help but laugh too. "You could never let me win."

"Because your will is weak, my lady," Jeff blurted out.

Terri frowned a bit. "You said that on our third date."

"Which led to—"

"The birth of our child."

There was an awkward silence as the two took a moment to remember the good times. Something had to be said, a new topic needed to be explored. Terri coughed. "I'm so sorry to hear about Ida."

Jeff closed his eyes. He was hoping that wouldn't come up. Terri didn't want Amanda attending the funeral, and Jeff tried his best to argue with her to let Amanda come with him. However, this time Terri won that argument. The funeral was four days ago, and he still was struggling with the loss of his second wife. "The police stopped by the house," Jeff said, not making eye contact. "They think I killed her."

"But you didn't. You were nowhere near the hospital when she died."

"Exactly."

The appetizers came. Terri could practically hear the hunger screaming out her name. Before the waiter stepped away from the table, Jeff ordered the salad Terri was craving and he ordered lunch for himself. By the time he was done ordering, she was now reconsidering her lunch choice. The thought of parmesan crusted lamb nearly distracted her enough to stop talking about Ida's sudden passing. She picked up one of the chicken bites and popped it in her mouth. She moaned.

"Shit, this is really good. What kind of breading is this?" she asked, picking up another piece and dipping it in the sauce on the middle of the plate.

"It's a three-cheese blend, basically," Jeff responded as he took a piece and ate one. "But I'm not revealing any more than that."

"Amanda would love this," she murmured as she took another from the plate.

"She does," Jeff admitted. "I made this about two weeks ago? Can't remember."

"And that's why I'm here," Terri said, taking the napkin and wiping her mouth. "Jeff, I'm really worried about her."

He looked up at her. She was nervously picking at the napkin, and he couldn't blame her. He had seen the odd change happening in his daughter. Terri began to explain how she had seen Amanda cut one of the stuffed animals and Jeff nearly dropped his glass of water.

"Are you thinking about having a doctor check her out?" asked Jeff.

"It wouldn't hurt. Has she been acting weird at your place?"

He was expecting her to ask that question. He cleared his throat. "It's weird how attached she is to that toy you got her for Christmas. She's always with the dog and talking to it. But the funny thing is, she lost the dog a few times."

"How can you lose a toy you've become obsessive over?" Terri genuinely asked. She couldn't fathom Amanda being away from the toy.

"Good question. But when she loses the toy, it's like something comes over her. She's a completely different little girl. She gets angry – no, not angry – she gets in these fits of rage."

"What exactly is she doing?"

"She's knocked things over. The other day, she broke my

grandmother's portrait because 'she didn't like the way she smiled.' Of course, I grounded her. I didn't like what I had to do, but when I dragged her into her room as punishment, she threw a bunch of words I didn't even think she knew."

"Oh, come on Jeff," Terri scolded. "She's heard those words from her classmates. You know as well as I do that kids are not perfect angels."

"Point taken," Jeff said as the waiter brought their lunches to the table, setting it before them. The waiter was a very handsome gentleman. In his hands, he was holding one of those fancy pepper grinders Delana purred over at the kitchen store in the mall. Both of them asked for a light dust of pepper on their dinners. Terri looked at Jeff's plate regretfully.

"Greg, can you bring me a smaller plate, please?" Jeff asked the waiter.

"Sure thing, Boss."

Terri looked at the waiter and then stole a glance at Jeff, who couldn't help but grin like an idiot. "Boss?"

Immediately, Jeff began to blush. "Not to take away from the main conversation, but I may have gotten a promotion."

"That's wonderful!"

They lifted up their water glasses in congratulations. Terri was super pleased with what was happening with Jeff, to the point where she nearly forgot about the subject at hand.

"Thanks, honey," Jeff said, turning back to his lamb. The waiter came back with a small plate. Jeff dished up a spoonful of garlic mashed potatoes and a good amount of lamb onto the plate, pushing it closer to her.

She took a bite of the lamb and Jeff gave her one of his "hey now" looks. "You're supposed to dip the lamb into the potato."

"Garlic parmesan taste, right?" Terri grinned.

"Exactly. Take another bite, but please do it correctly," he said, grinning.

Terri obeyed her ex-husband's command and knew

exactly why she was supposed to eat the lamb in that way. "Okay. I admit it. I'm an idiot."

"Much better, isn't it?"

"Ten times better. Jeff, I hate to say this but as good as Delana cooks, you have her beat by more than a mile."

"Really?" Jeff blushed again.

"Don't tell her I said that."

Without thinking, Jeff leaned forward and kissed Terri. He missed her lips, kissing her on the cheek.

"Jeff," Terri said reprovingly. She wasn't too surprised at Jeff's kiss, but at the same time, she was almost wanting him to kiss her.

She didn't know why she felt the way she did.

"Sorry. I shouldn't have done that," Jeff said, looking away and going back to his lunch. "For a moment, it was like we were married again, you sittin' at the dinner table like an expectant child excited for dinner."

"Those were good times, yes I agree, but you really shouldn't have tried to kiss me."

They went back to their meals, not talking for a while. It was just two people sitting together. Anyone who may have known them would have figured they were just there, talking about life and catching up on each other's affairs. But something about that kiss they might have witnessed would have seen a yearning in both of them.

Especially Terri. They would have seen it the most in her eyes.

-9-

Something did not quite make sense to Detective Mickey Adams as he thought back on the visit he and his partner made to Jeff Toms' house. Both of them had the sinking feeling they weren't talking to the murderer at all, but when they walked in the house, they had the oddest thought that the murderer was there, lurking somewhere inside. It was just a house call to inform him of Ida Toms' passing, even though they were still very much suspicious they were talking to the murderer himself.

At first, Jeff didn't believe them. He thought that it was some sick, practical joke lined up by Ida. But the longer he listened to them, the longer he stood before them, grief overwhelmed him. Knees buckling from the weight of his internal anguish, he took a seat.

After talking with Jeff for at least fifteen minutes, they learned more about Ida Toms. Reflecting back on that meeting, it became clearer to Mickey that there could have been some other possible suspect out there. But there was that nagging suspicion the murderer was in the house.

It was enough to follow that gut feeling and make another house call. Maybe the two of them could do a follow-up, just to look around the residence and see if there were any hints as to what really happened. Even though she was not killed in the house, there was always the possibility something in the house would reveal something to them. Is it possible that the killer knew both of them, if the suspect wasn't Jeff at all?

Yes. It is.

Mickey looked over at his partner in the car as they drove back to the Toms' house. "What are you hoping to find?"

He always asked Ian this question when they headed to someone's home. Ian thought about it for a second as he took a drink of his stale coffee. He made a face and cleared his throat, trying to eradicate the taste of the drink from his mouth. "Something that will bring us closer to the murderer. Jeff talked about a brother of hers. Maybe…?"

"I don't think so," replied Mickey. "But it's something to look into."

"She probably has a personal phone book somewhere lying around," said Ian, thinking out loud, not necessarily expecting any kind of response from his partner. "Probably a diary or something."

"We'll take it into evidence, if there is one," said Mickey as they pulled to the front of the house. Jeff's vehicle was in the driveway. He was home.

Just as they were about to walk to the door, Ian quickly ran back to the patrol car for the warrant papers. He always forgot to take them in hand, leaving it against his coffee mug. Shaking his head, he grabbed it and joined his partner. Jeff had already opened the door at this point.

"…a warrant?" Ian heard Jeff ask as he approached from behind.

"It's possible your wife knew her murderer. Since you refused us access to her personal belongings when we were here the first time, we need to look to see if there is anything that may be helpful for this investigation," said Mickey as Ian handed the warrant papers to a very upset mourner.

"I'm sorry about that," replied Jeff. "It was an absolute shock for me. Yes, take whatever you think you need."

Ian couldn't help but agree with the man and remarked

so, genuine compassion leaving his lips. He knew that if he were in the situation, he would want some time to think things over, to gloss things over. It was as though a deceased person's personal belongings actually became that person, in some sense. Or, at least, ended up attracting the soul of the departed.

He didn't quite believe in ghosts and stuff like that, but a part of him wondered if there was life after death. It was that Catholic upbringing of his that first sparked the curiosity of a real life after death. More and more people were starting to share their experiences with the unexplainable – it was fascinating but there was always the insinuation that a logical explanation could be found.

The two detectives made their way into the master bedroom. Clothes were thrown in a hamper sitting next to a dresser, but the floor also played host to numerous polos and a few jeans. The dresser top was an array of various items, most of which probably belonged to Jeff. As they drew nearer to the dresser, it became clear that most of them belonged to the late Ida Toms. An unclean foundation brush threatened to fall off the dresser and Mickey was tempted to push it back to keep it from dropping. He looked around curiously at the dresser, hoping to see something that would be of some use.

Unless he wanted to paint his face with foundation and coat his nails green, Mickey was out of luck. He moved away from the dresser and toward the nightstand on the right of the California Queen-sized bed. There were two of them, one he supposed Ida used when she slept next to her husband. The bed wasn't made. Pillows were angled in a mess on the top of the bed, pushing into the headboard shelves housing various knick-knacks. Mickey smiled at the little soldier statue on the top center. It reminded him of the one he had in his living room. A few watches were scattered in random places and an alarm clock sat on the edge, its red lights bright and loud.

The top of the dresser he was next to was empty, save for a romance novel. Ignoring the book, he opened the single drawer and found a few items inside. Tucked in the corner was a little blue journal. Gloves on, he gingerly picked the book up and placed it in the evidence bag. A small pamphlet was underneath where he retrieved the journal. He frowned. Since this was clearly Ida's nightstand, he felt bad that she suffered from a disease that had taken his sister from him about six years ago. He shook his head. "Our deceased woman was an alcoholic," he finally said to his partner.

"How do you know that?"

Mickey held up the pamphlet. "It's an AA brochure. Twelve steps. Poor woman."

Ian mournfully swore under his breath. His eyes glanced at the bag holding the blue, spiraled journal. "What else did you find?"

"It's a journal," answered Mickey, matter-of-factly. "We can look at it later. There might be some other stuff lying around that will prove to be helpful."

"You gonna check the headboard?"

"There's not a lot there, but it'd be worth it to take a look around."

Mickey took his time, glancing at each section of the bookcase headboard. There wasn't anything that really stuck out to him. A few small books were lying down, their spines unaligned, revealing a person who had literary inclinations toward thrillers and splatterpunk. It was somewhat suspicious, but for a moment he couldn't help but appreciate Jeff's taste in books. The ones Jeff owned were ones he read a few years back and thoroughly enjoyed, even though he was not much of a reader now.

As he moved to the center, he saw something red sticking out from one of the golden-colored pillows. Angling his head, he pulled it out from its location. It looked exactly the same as the one he had seen in the hospital room.

Jeff appeared in the doorway to the room. He looked at

the two, hesitating for a brief second. "Um, how much longer d'you guys think you'll be? I need to get my daughter soon."

"We're close to being done," said Mickey, not looking at him. "I think we have everything we need, but I'm glad you came in here. Have you seen this before?" Mickey held the ribbon between his gloved fingers.

Jeff walked closer to the ribbon. "It kinda looks like the ribbon on my daughter's stuffed dog."

"Is that toy in your daughter's room, sir?"

Jeff stiffened up. "I don't think that's really necessary, Detective. That's my daughter's toy and she has it with her."

"She brings the toy to school with her?" asked Ian.

"Yes. My ex-wife gifted that to Amanda on Christmas," explained Jeff, his voice gradually rising with suspicion and annoyance. Then he realized that maybe he shouldn't drag them into this. They're going to want to talk to both of them. "You can't pull her away from it."

Mickey looked over to Ian briefly before making eye contact with Jeff. "Don't worry. We won't take the toy, but we do need to look at it."

"For what reason?"

"This ribbon is the same ribbon we found on your deceased wife's hospital bed," said Mickey, frowning. "You do know this doesn't look good for you."

It wasn't a question.

Jeff smiled; his lips pursed in obvious irritation. "So I suppose I have to find someone else to pick my daughter up."

Mickey paused for a moment. "Pick your daughter up. But one of us will be coming with you." He looked over at his partner.

"Sure thing," replied Ian.

"She's gonna ask what you're doing in my car, you know," Jeff said to Ian, not wanting the passenger.

"Just say that I'm a friend who happens to work for the cops." Ian walked over to Jeff and stopped next to him. "We don't need to make it any more awkward than it needs to be."

Mickey could swear he heard Jeff sigh in irritation as they left the room, leaving him alone in the house. As they walked out, he wondered if Jeff was lying to them all along. But why bring a little child into this whole mess? Was there something else going on, something even more nefarious than a simple murder?

JEFF HAD NEVER seen Amanda act the way she had before. And he certainly did not want that to be the last thing he remembered of his daughter. Now he was Suspect Number One. That damned ribbon implicated him!

But it wasn't there before. He would have seen it.

Wouldn't he have?

What was it even doing there?

When the detectives forced his daughter to show the toy, which took much longer than it really should have, the ribbon Mickey had in the evidence bag was identical to the toy's ribbon tied to its paw, if not the very same ribbon in terms of size and width. The detectives were great in dealing with her, but he was very much unimpressed with Amanda's sheer lack of understanding and attention to the situation. She almost fought the poor detective who wanted to take the toy into evidence.

Eventually they decided to just take a picture. He knew he should have just yanked it out of her hands, but something stopped him from doing so. And he saw that same restriction come over the eyes of the two detectives standing before her. It was peculiar. There was something that came over him, something physically stopping himself from removing the fucking toy from Amanda's firm grip. Even the grip she had on the toy seemed supernatural to him. She wasn't that tough, wasn't that stone cold.

It wasn't his daughter.

He had called Terri before the police finally took him in

for further questioning. When she arrived at the house, Jeff briefly explained what was happening and that she had to take Amanda for a period of time. Typically, she would have been thrilled to spend more time with her daughter, but something in her eyes caught his attention. It was as though she didn't want Amanda with her. There was a haunting fear in her eyes.

She cut off one of the tentacles, Jeff. And she was grinning like a maniac while she did it.

With the sudden change in Amanda's whole personality and everything else in between, Jeff became frightened. He suddenly wondered if staying at Terri's place was such a good idea. Maybe she needs to stay at a children's hospital for a time?

If she's capable of destroying toys he knows she loves, what else was she capable of? As much as Jeff was curious, another part of him did not want that question answered.

SHE COULDN'T GET herself to say anything to her daughter as they drove away from Jeff's house. As she neared their home, Terri felt nervous. The questions the detectives asked her hogged her mind. They wanted to know everything about the toy. They wanted to know where she found it. She told them exactly all that she knew – the dog was a donation by someone to be sold at her antique store. She told them that Amanda really wanted a stuffed dog. She told them that the other things the woman handed off to her had already been sold. Then there was an obsessive four minutes where the detectives asked her why she kept records when it wasn't necessary. She briefly explained that she knew of another woman who owned an antique store and was implicated in a crime involving stolen items. Terri wanted to be vigilant, wanted to be prepared should something insane happen like that to her and her business.

Even though she knew it wouldn't, it was always best to

be prepared for any circumstances. Her grandfather taught her that life-lesson.

"Always be prepared, Care-Bear," she could hear him say days before he succumbed to lung cancer.

They wanted to know exactly who it was that brought those things into the antique store. Since she was the only one in the area who required donors to fill out paperwork, it was easy to pull that out from the records and make a copy for the detectives.

She just didn't want to.

But she knew if she didn't, she would be withholding evidence. She would be letting a killer go. And she knew deep in her heart that Jeff did not kill his wife. She knew he did not kill Ida. He was innocent.

But why? The woman who had given those things away wasn't exactly the nicest woman in the world. But it was the only answer Terri had. Somehow, the donation woman was connected to the killing of Ida Toms. A huge part of Terri was more curious than a mouse on the hunt for cheese.

She couldn't remember the woman's name, but she knew that she received those items close to Christmas time, which would make things easy when she went to retrieve the documentation.

Amanda ran into the house and Terri slowly followed behind her. Delana was sitting in the kitchen, nursing a hot cup of tea, reading a magazine. She looked up and watched as Amanda rushed into her room, closing the door rather harshly. She went back to her magazine. Terri wanted to go after her, to talk to her about what was about to happen but thought that maybe she should wait a few hours.

Or a few days.

Delana stared at Terri as she joined her at the table. "What happened?"

"He's basically at the station, being questioned by some idiot detectives," Terri said furiously. "You'll never guess what they wanted to do."

"Who?" asked Delana, her eyes still fixated on something in the magazine she was reading.

"The detectives, Delana," Terri snapped. "Stay with me here."

"Sorry," she said quickly.

Terri explained how the detectives thought that Jeff was responsible for Ida's murder. She explained that there was a red ribbon left on the hospital bed, as well as on Jeff's, and the ribbon was basically the same as the one on the toy. As Terri finished telling Delana about everything, Delana shook her head in disgust.

"They honestly think he has red ribbons lying around and leaves them next to dead bodies? That's ridiculous!"

Terri snorted disdainfully. "So then I explained that I found the toy at the antique store and now they want to go through my records. They want to know who brought those things to the store."

"Okay?" Delana scratched at an itch on her arm with her long nails. "So why bring Jeff in, when they are clearly second-guessing who the murderer is?"

"Because he was the one who had access to the toy."

"You can't get that thing away from Amanda."

"And that's another thing, too," said Terri. She told Delana about how her little girl had acted, according to the detectives.

"There's something really wrong with her," said Delana, not thinking about what she was saying. Terri glared at her.

"What do you mean by that?"

"She's acting very differently, and I know you can see it, too," whispered Delana, as though Amanda could hear her.

Terri closed her eyes. Delana was right. There *was* something horrifically wrong with Amanda. She had never gotten so obsessive over any of her toys in the past. She was seriously considering finding a doctor that dealt with this kind of thing. "You think she's ill?"

Delana got up from where she was sitting to refill her cup

with hot water. Grabbing a tea bag, she began to stoop the tea in the water. "I think," she began, trying to find the best words to say, "I think that it wouldn't hurt to have her examined by a child psychiatrist."

Terri bit her lower lip. "I have been planning on it."

"Better get on it, before this all explodes in your face, honey," she said, going back to the table. "I don't think it would hurt to have someone look her over. There's got to be a reason for all this."

"What do you think is the reason? Because I've thought long and hard about this, and I can't think of shit!"

Then it dawned on her. The answer was right in her face, and for some strange reason, it hit her like a ton of bricks that she willingly let happen.

"Ida," both of them replied in unison.

"I DON'T THINK I've ever seen such a more beautiful toy before, Amanda," said Dr. Tobi, fondly looking at the stuffed dog. "Can you tell me where you got it?"

Amanda eyed the doctor suspiciously. "Why?"

"I think it's very cute," the doctor said to her. "My daughter would love to have one of her own."

Amanda pursed her lips. "She won't be able to find one like this," she said icily.

"What makes you say that?"

"My mother found it. At her store. It has old stuff. Stuff that people hate and don't want anymore."

"You think that the person who brought it into your mommy's store hates the toy?"

Amanda laughed, but it wasn't out of amusement. "It's *mother*, stupid."

"That's not nice to call someone you just met 'stupid,' you know," said Dr. Tobi. "What makes you think I'm stupid?"

"Because you're asking really stupid questions, stupid."

Dr. Tobi smiled empathetically at Amanda. She was used

to this kind of talk from some of her patients. "That's a very hurtful thing to say. But I'm a big girl. I can take it. Can you tell me why you think the person who brought that into your mother's store hates the toy?"

"It's a reminder," said Amanda. She brought the toy to her ears as though it was saying something to her. "It brings bad memories to her."

"What kind of bad memories?"

"I can't tell you," said Amanda.

Dr. Tobi looked in Amanda's eyes. There was something there that made her even more curious about this little girl sitting in the playroom with her. Amanda wasn't interested in any of the other things in the room. She attempted to have Amanda use crayons, but she threw them across the room. She tried something with puppets, but Amanda kept yawning and saying how bored she was. Instead of trying anything new, she just went back to tradition: Let Amanda do what she wants and allow her to open up that way.

"Is it something bad?" pursued Dr. Tobi.

"Very bad," whispered Amanda.

"Can you give me a hint?"

Amanda looked strangely at the doctor. "Why?"

"Because this toy is very special to you. I had a toy that was very special to me when I was a kid and we shared everything. And if I knew someone hurt my toy, someone should know, too. They could help the toy process what happened, and it could get healthy again."

Amanda smiled, but this time Dr. Tobi could tell it was genuine. "Okay. I want my toy to be shrunk."

Dr. Tobi couldn't hold in a chuckle. "So, what happened to the toy?"

Amanda looked at the toy, holding it back up against her ear again. She looked at the kind woman in front of her. "She has a poem for you. Violet Red wants to tell you her favorite poem."

"I like poems," lied Dr. Tobi. "I'd love to hear it."

Amanda's smile went away. "Violet Red says you're lying."

"Why does Violet Red think I'm lying?"

"Because she knows you don't like poems. You failed your high school English class because you struggled with poetry. And you had a teacher that—"

Dr. Tobi couldn't hide her surprise. There was no way she could have known that. "In school, you read a lot of things that you don't like, because the teacher wants you to enjoy them and know what they are saying. You're right. I didn't like English, and I did fail one class because it was a very hard class. But I'd still like to hear—"

Something fell off the shelf. Dr. Tobi looked behind her and found a bucket of toy bricks had fallen down. She'd pick it up later, but she knew that the container was nowhere close to the edge.

"Violet Red is mad at you," Amanda whispered.

"Oh? Did I do something bad?"

"You lied."

Dr. Tobi faked a cough, leaning forward so that she could look into the dog's eyes. It was almost comical, but it would be very beneficial for the little girl sitting before her. She was willing to do anything to get Amanda to open up more. "Violet Red, I'm very sorry for lying to you about liking poems. You're right – I don't. But I still would love to hear your poem. If you'll still let me hear it."

There was a brief pause as Amanda looked the doctor over. She smiled again. "Violet Red says she's sorry for knocking over your toy bricks. And she's sad that your English teacher hurt you in your asshole. She wants you to feel better, so she wants to tell you her poem, to make you feel better."

To keep Amanda from seeing her face go pale, Dr. Tobi looked back at the bucket. Turning her head back to her patient, she told her she was ready to hear the poem, doing her best to keep herself from losing her sanity.

How did she know that?

How did a little girl, who she met for the very first time today, know that her high school English teacher assaulted her? The mere mention of this little girl so casually bringing up the most traumatic moment in her life – which had caused so much depression and a shit-ton of anxiety – made the hair on the back of her neck and her arms prickle. She could even still feel the pain between her legs.

Keep your focus.

It's okay.

Breathe.

The little girl sitting before her gave a sympathetic smile. "Violet Red says you're not ready to hear the poem."

Dr. Tobi stared at the stuffed animal, sitting comfortably on the girl's lap. "What makes Violet Red think I'm not ready?"

"Can I leave now?" Amanda suddenly asked. There was something in her eyes that took Dr. Tobi back. She looked frightened.

"Just a few more minutes left," Dr. Tobi remarked, looking up at the clock. There were about five more minutes left of the therapy session. "Maybe you could write—"

Amanda suddenly stood up, staring Dr. Tobi down, and let out the most ear-piercing scream she had ever heard. This little girl didn't seem like a little girl anymore. The fear that was in her eyes a second ago was replaced by rage. Within just a few seconds, her mother came rushing into the therapy room. It was difficult to control the girl. She fought against her mother for at least a full minute. Then, as though something was controlling her, Amanda fell limp to the floor. Terri picked her up, looking very bemused and glared at Dr. Tobi.

"I think we're done here," said Terri. "Thank you for this, but clearly this is too much for her."

"This might be a bit out of my reach," said Dr. Tobi, reaching for her pad and pen. "I'm going to have to recommend she sees a doctor that is more… umm." She stumbled through her words. What she had just witnessed was something she had never seen in her professional career, and she thought she had seen it all. "Someone more qualified. I know someone who could be a better fit for her."

"I don't know," said Terri, close to whispering. Amanda was still limp in her arms. "I don't know. I imagine this session is going to cost an arm and a leg as it is."

Dr. Tobi swallowed hard. "Your daughter needs treatment. I'm very concerned. You saw what happened in here. Please, at least give him a call," she said, handing the small sheet of paper over. Terri acknowledged it before sticking it in her coat pocket.

"When we get home, yes," murmured Terri.

She began to head out of the room. Right before she left, Dr. Tobi grabbed her lightly by the arm. "Are you a religious woman?"

Terri turned her head, smirking, her eyebrows wrinkling in confusion. "A woman like me is shamed for even walking into a church, Dr. Tobi. Why do you ask?"

"It was silly. I'm sorry for even considering the notion," Dr. Tobi replied back, letting her arms drop to her sides. "It's just… well, my cousin is a Catholic priest… he's shared stuff that he's witness—"

Terri's smirk grew wider. "Are you saying my daughter's…" She couldn't get herself to finish the sentence. The invisible words were too hard to ignore.

"No, no of course not. That's the stuff of fiction," Dr. Tobi said quickly. "I do think, from a professional standpoint, that there may be a psychological relief from that kind of thing, you know, exorcisms. That's all."

"There may be?" Terri asked, eyeing the doctor suspiciously.

"Forget I mentioned it. But I do think your daughter needs immediate treatment. Promise me you'll call the other doctor?"

"Of course," said Terri as they finally left her office.

SHE WAS GREETED by the detectives the moment she walked into her store. She forgot she was supposed to meet them earlier – the craziness she witnessed at Dr. Tobi's office was still on her mind. She played with the paper in her pocket as she dropped Amanda off at her father's. Her daughter needed help. It was very clear to her.

"I'm so sorry," she said to them apologetically, rummaging through her file cabinet. "I had to bring my daughter to an appointment."

"It's no problem, ma'am," one of the detectives responded warmly.

Terri didn't respond back. She found the file that had the donor's information on it and made a copy of it. She handed it off to the bulkier detective – Mickey, was it? She couldn't remember his name.

"Thank you," the detective said, glancing at the paper. "Has she donated before?"

"No, I've never seen her before," replied Terri. "She seemed very rushed and didn't even want to fill that out."

"Not a very clear writer, is she?" said the detective, pressing his lips together in irritation.

"At least the address is clear," the other responded back.

"Do you think she has something to do with Ida's death?" Terri asked Mickey.

"We don't know," Mickey said while Ian took a glance at the things in the store. "But the stuffed dog was in the woman's possession. It is likely that, if she made that toy herself, that she has more of that ribbon lying around."

"But anyone could have the same material in their homes," Terri found herself saying. She wasn't trying to defend the rude woman, but she couldn't believe this woman could have murdered a complete stranger!

"True," Ian replied, turning around to face Terri. "But

this is an investigation. And quite honestly, we don't have much to go on, aside from that red ribbon connected to Ida Toms' murder and your daughter's toy."

"Right, of course," said Terri as she closed the filing cabinet. "I really hope you find the bastard who did this."

"You weren't on good terms with Ida, were you?" asked Mickey very suddenly.

Terri's eyes went wide. "Excuse me?"

"Just answer the question, ma'am."

The way he said *ma'am* nearly pissed her off. It was so demeaning, and it felt very disrespectful. The word *ma'am* made her feel much older than she was. It sounded so derogatory. She sneered at Mickey, speaking slowly as though she were talking to a child diagnosed with a learning disability. "How do you think you'd feel if you found out your ex's new wife was verbally abusing your daughter?"

"I'd be pissed, too," remarked Ian, ignoring Terri's agitation.

For a moment there was silence, apart from a regular customer who showed up every week. Terri glanced at the woman as she picked up a couple of items. Looking back at the detectives, she said out-right that she didn't kill Ida. She had no idea she was even at the hospital.

The customer smiled over at Terri and lifted up an item that wasn't priced. She was mentally disabled and struggled with reading the room, but for a brief second she pretended as though it was just her and the customer.

Detective Mickey broke the fantasy. "We'll let you get back to business," he said as he regarded the customer. Terri had a sinking feeling that he was judging the woman as she continued to haphazardly throw things in a shopping basket. Terri flinched as the woman continued to do this, even though she knew that the woman did not know any better, no matter how hard she attempted to correct her. She wondered where the woman's guardian was. Sometimes he was with her, but today was the exception.

"Ma'am, can I give you a hand?" asked Ian as he flashed the woman with a compassionate, kind smile.

In broken English, the woman replied, "My things. In basket." She gestured at a small tea set. Ian seemed to understand what the woman was trying to say.

"Yes, you have very beautiful things," he said as he looked over at Terri and grabbed the tea set, setting it carefully in the basket. Immediately, Terri's respect of the detective went up. "Do you like tea?"

"I drink tea," she responded.

"What's your favorite?"

"The one that look like coffee."

"Black tea?"

The woman nodded her head vigorously.

Ian smiled and patted her on the shoulder. The woman responded by putting a hand where the detective touched her and smiled back at him as he walked back up to the register. "I like you," she said as he took out a ten-dollar bill and placed it on the counter. Terri's eyes grew huge.

"You don't have to—"

"Please," Ian said, placing his wallet in his back pocket. "I want to."

Terri mouthed a thank you as the men left her store. In all her time living and working here, she had never seen that kind of caring and generosity before. It gave her hope for a brighter world.

THE NEIGHBORHOOD THE detectives had entered was not an ideal area of the town, generally speaking. It seemed as though every day there was something going on, whether it was a domestic abuse situation, or a robbery gone wrong. Mickey hated it, but he couldn't help but admit this neighborhood was something of a kind of job security for him. Ian didn't mind the neighborhood, but a man in his position certainly had several reservations about going there.

Even though it was the daytime, the neighborhood gave a kind of feeling that it was nighttime 24/7. Ian cursed under his breath about the poor living conditions of these residents. They deserved much better, but the town officials couldn't care less about these people. Ian knew that if the conditions improved, if the residents had better access to services, that crime would go down.

But those sitting in their $1000 office chairs could care less about whether or not Joe Shmoe could afford electricity. They could care less if Marge couldn't afford bread and milk for her three sons.

Ian looked down at the form the woman had signed. "Beatrice? Betty? I can't make out the name."

"There should be some kind of requirement when you leave high school, that you write your name and contact information clearly," Mickey said in agreement.

"Agreed," Ian replied, looking at the small house before their eyes. "At least we know we're here. 1118 Sunset."

Mickey took the form out of Ian's hand. "Maybe it's Bessie?"

Ian noticed the faded green car pull into the driveway. "I guess we'll find out soon enough."

The woman who left the car had on a brightly colored shirt that was clearly not her size. Part of her belly was hanging low as she opened the backseat and pulled out what looked like groceries, her backside revealing more than the detectives needed to witness. She sat a bag down on the ground and hiked her pants up, but they fell back in place. She sighed loudly and muttered something about stores not carrying her size. As she took the other two bags, she noticed Ian and Mickey walking over to her.

Ian offered to help her bring the bags into the house. The woman looked at him, then let out a contentious laugh.

"You think I can't handle these myself?" the woman asked scornfully.

Ian was surprised at the woman's response. "No, not at

all. I was just—"

"You were just what? I can handle my groceries just fine. What do you want?"

Mickey was the one to speak, which was probably a bad call on his part. "Did you donate a few items to TerriRific Antiques in December?"

"They wasn't stolen, if that's what you was hinting at," she retorted back. "I'm not talking to you." She snapped her head over to Ian. "Or to you."

"We just have a question about one of those items, ma'am," said Ian. "I promise that we won't take up any more time than necessary."

The woman let out a very derisive laugh. "Oh. 'You won't take up no more time than nec'sary,' Sure." She laughed again.

"Actually, he's more so just tagging along with me. We're off duty," Ian lied, knowing fully well that he could get in trouble. Thankfully Mickey knew his shtick and knew it was extremely beneficial for this situation. "My little girl is about five and she's friends with another little girl who got a stuffed dog with the most beautiful red ribbon tied to its leg. Well, Mandy's really jealous and she told me she needs to have a toy just like that, or she will die." Ian laughed amusedly, but he was more so laughing because of how ridiculous his lie was.

The woman regarded Ian for a moment. To both Mickey and Ian's surprise, she bought it. Immediately, her countenance changed. "Mandy, huh? Beautiful name."

"She's a beautiful girl and she deserves the best, and I hear you're the best at making toys."

"I judged y'all wrong. I'm sorry. It's been such a hard time lately, what with my sister missin' and everythin'."

"Your sister's missing?" Mickey asked.

"Just up an' left," the woman affirmed. "I told her right before things went south that he was no good. He'd fin' her and shoot her. She took my advice, yeah, but I know

Lynnette. She'd tells me. She'd tells me!"

Ian asked, "Can you tell us what happened?"

The woman looked stunned. "I jus' told ya. I'm the first person she'd tell anyone if she was gon' leave. Had an abusive, conniving twat for a fiancé. They's stayed wit me for a week 'fore he foun' out and pulled her hair and tried to force her back to 'is place. But she, oh!" the woman laughed as if she was recollecting a humorous memory. "She grabbed that baseball bat behin' you and slugged him REAL good. Now, he was surprised as Hell and took off like he were a baseball flyin' outta left field. Threatened to come back, that piece of shit. But he never did."

Suddenly, a look of epiphany came over her face. "That piece of shit!"

She looked gravely stricken. Mickey coughed. "Do you think he killed your sister?"

Instead of responding, she picked up a ceramic ashtray and threw it against the wall. "That piece of shit!"

Ian held up a hand, worried she might end up slugging one of them. "Let's not throw things. We don't want you to get hurt."

She turned over to them, a curious, frightening pink lipped grin staring into their eyes. "Biff Harder. That's 'is name. Biff Harder."

Biff Harder.

Mickey recognized the name. Other officers had picked him up several times for breaking and entering. He wasn't surprised Biff was the man. But at the same time, he didn't think Biff was a killer. He was more of a drug addict than anything else.

The two detectives exchanged a glance. Their eyes said it all – what they thought was a simple murder case might end up being something bigger. They just weren't certain just how big the case would be. Mickey hoped that if they found Biff Harder, that it would end the whole thing. Take in the man in for domestic abuse and that would solve the whole thing! He asked the woman if he knew where Harder was and she gladly gave him his address.

Ian suddenly remembered about the red ribbon. To get her to calm down a bit, he said, "So, you make your own toys. That's a very commendable job, if you ask me."

The woman's chest puffed out a little more, forgetting entirely about her sudden burst of rage. She smiled. "You see that there stuffed bear on the mantle?"

Ian nodded. It was a beautiful toy for his fake daughter.

"Stuffed it myself. Tied the ribbon myself. Isn't it something?"

"You have a talent, that's for sure," Ian said, returning the smile. "I assume you made one for your niece?"

"Sure did. It was a stuffed dog I had crafted not even a week before she went missin'," she replied.

"Would you happen to have that toy?"

"Nah," she said, tears forming in her eyes. "I couldn't bear to look at it, or the other things belonging to my sister and niece. I know they wouldn't come back with Biff hangin' around, so I donated them."

-10-

Tracking down Biff Harder wasn't an easy task. The thirty-five-year-old African American had been evicted from his apartment only about two weeks ago and the one homeless shelter in town had no record of him staying. The man was homeless and could be anywhere. It took a few days, but they finally tracked him down at a park, feeding the birds and drinking something Ian knew wasn't water. The five-foot, seven-inch man was clearly drunk. He didn't look homeless – his clothes smelled like he had just sprayed cologne and looked freshly cleaned.

"These birds will eat jus' about anythin' you give 'em," he said as they sat down next to him on the park bench. "They really like day-ol' bran muffins. You ever notice how the birds guzzle up that food?"

"When was the last time you ate anything, Mr. Harder?" asked Ian, watching the birds peck at the ground.

"Aw, it's not me who needs the feedin', sir," he said as he took another drink of his vodka.

"You look starved," Ian responded.

"I's fine, thanks."

Ian gave Mickey a quick glance. Mickey knew that look. He headed to the car and begrudgingly pulled out the other half of his sandwich. Coming back to the bench, he offered it to Biff. To his surprise, Biff took it gratefully and began to eat it very slowly, appreciating and savoring the food.

"I thought you said you weren't hungry," Ian said, smiling.

"When you's offered a sammich, you take it," he said in between bites.

Ian couldn't help but chuckle. "Can you tell me a little bit about Lynnette and her daughter?"

Biff slowly put the sandwich on his lap and looked at Ian, dead in the eyes. "She don't listen much to me. I jus' wanted her back, but that sister of hers gets in her head way too offen."

"You guys didn't get along very well?" asked Ian. Mickey was basically nothing more than a fixture on the bench at that point. He knew when Ian needed to take the wheel, and he was the best at connecting with people in a way Mickey couldn't.

He didn't know what he would do without him.

"Oh, we gots along just fine. Fine pussy. Best sex ever. But she got miffed after I tol' her that her sister was a-lyin' and that I didn't steal nuttin' from nobody. You give that woman a fine bracelet and she throws it back at ya, cuz she think you rob some white-ass motherfucker instead of doin' things the right way. So, I react like any man who would be accused of doin' somethin' he didn't do."

"And what did you do, Mr. Harder?"

"You know somethin'?" Biff turned around to face the detective. "I like you."

"Please, Mr. Harder," Ian replied. "What did you do?"

"I lost my temper at her," he said tonelessly. "I been drinkin' an' I see my hand swattin' at her face. And she freaks out and drags Violet out of the house. Went to her sister's. But you know somethin'?"

"What?"

"I regret it, yessir. I regret it. But the red just overwhelm me an' I stew in my hatred an' I drink an' it possesses me. I wait a bit, I did. An' I let that rage fester inside my blood an' next thing I knows, I'm at Bea's with some welts on my body an' it hurt like a motherfucking bitch."

"You were hit?" Mickey asked suddenly, causing Ian to jump. For a moment he forgot his partner was with him.

"Yessir, I was hit by a baseball bat. I ain't no baseball!"

"And then what happened?"

"I knowed what I did was wrong, so I's left. Never came back, no I didn't."

"Do you know what happened to Lynnette and her daughter – you called her Violet?"

"Funny name, if ya ask me. She ain't no white girl. She 'bout as black as I am."

"Is she your daughter?" asked Mickey.

"Nah," he said. "She had that girl long before I knowed her."

He leaned over to his side, barely an inch away from Ian's ear. "I think somethin' else happened. I do."

"What do you think happened to them?"

Biff looked down at the sandwich, tore off the bread and threw it down on the ground. A couple birds came out of a tree and began pecking at the wheat. He threw the remainder of the naked sandwich into his mouth and began chewing.

Mickey repeated the question, a little more irritated that his sandwich was wasted on some stupid birds.

"They dabble in things they shouldn't be," he responded back. "Las' time I saw that little girl, she was with her mama and there were these black candles."

Ian looked over at Mickey.

"They was sayin' somethin', readin' somethin' outta some book. Didn't sound an inch like any English I knows. An' I look over at what's between them, an' it's a toy. An' I see a photograph of myself there, too!"

In a hushed voice, he continued. "Ya just don't do that kin' of thing, you know? So I stop it. And they's got very real upset." He began to shudder, but he composed himself. "I cry out, 'Black magic – that's black magic!' an' they look at me real angry an' shit an' that's where things get a bit hazy for me. I don't recall what happen next, but I recall feelin' real sick to my stomach. They did somethin' to me, I knows they did."

"Did you drink anything? Did you eat something bad?" Mickey asked, not liking where this was going.

"Nah, sir. I didn't," Biff said, watching the birds again.

"Where do you think Lynnette and Violet ran off to? Do you have any idea?" asked Ian.

Biff thought really hard about the question. "I'm sure they're still at Bea's. I dunno," he said, sounding really uncomfortable.

"Do you happen to know a woman by the name of Ida Toms, by any chance?" asked Mickey.

Biff looked over at Mickey and laughed to himself. He looked over at Ian. "He don't focus too good, do he?"

Ian didn't answer the question.

"Yes, I knows that woman," Biff said, grinning. "I fucked her real good not long after my, ah, *thing* at Lynnette's."

Both of the detectives got up from the bench. Biff looked at them, confused. Then it hit him.

"Wait, what is this all about?" he asked them, getting up from the bench.

Without answering, Mickey grabbed his handcuffs. "Hands behind your back. You're under arrest for the murder of Ida Toms and the disappearance of Lynnette Redd and her daughter, Violet Redd. You have the right to an attorney…"

IF AMANDA HAD any say in who her classmates were, Briton and his brother Dexter wouldn't be allowed in the school. Out of all the kids in Miss Hammett's classroom, the two boys were the worst. They made fun of everybody and when they were out on the playground, away from Miss

Hammett, they were ten times worse.

She clutched the toy at her lap as she swayed back and forth on the swing set. She was hoping she would see her friend Vi again, but since December, she hadn't seen hair or chin of her. Maybe she goes to another school? she asked herself. Too afraid to ask her teacher about the little black girl who she met, she kept the girl a secret. She knew Briton and Dexter would probably call Vi bad names, names her mother said to never call someone who wasn't white. If she asked Miss Hammett about Vi, then one of the boys would hear and they'd pester and obsess until they found her.

She couldn't let that happen.

As she started to focus on her swinging, she felt someone push her off the swing.

"It's my turn," a boy's voice whined loudly. "Stop hogging the damn swings!"

Amanda straightened herself back up. Holding the dog next to her, she turned around to face Briton. "There's other swings, you know."

Briton leered at her. "Shut up. And what's that piece of shit you're holding on to?"

"You're not supposed to say that word."

Big mistake.

Briton leaped from the swing and thundered over to her. "What are you gonna do if I say it again?"

Before Amanda could respond, he kept repeating that bad word. When he finally stopped, he looked at the toy and snatched it out of her hand. Amanda gasped.

"This thing's fucking ugly," he said, pulling at the eyes. One of them popped off its face. He laughed maliciously as he threw it down on the ground and stomped on it. She looked at her once-beautiful toy. Her best friend. She glared at Briton as he picked the toy back up in his hands.

"You hurt Violet Red," she whispered.

"Violet Red?" Briton laughed. A few of the older kids walked over to where they were standing.

Aware of his audience, he turned his head over in their direction, held her toy as though it was about to be sacrificed, twisted the dog's head, threw it back down to the ground and shouted, "She calls this stupid thing, Violet Red!"

A few of the girls awkwardly laughed. Amanda couldn't help but think just how spineless and useless the older kids were. It infuriated her. But she also knew if they challenged him, they would have to deal with him. And Amanda couldn't blame them. Briton is a big kid – he could beat up those girls and walk away without a scratch.

"Violet Red!" he screeched. "Violet Fucking Red!" he laughed again.

"Hey!" a man's voice boomed from the side of the playground. "What's going on?"

Amanda closed her eyes. It was one of the playground monitors. She watched as Taylor approached them. He reminded her of a giant – he was even taller than most of the teachers she knew.

"I asked you two a question," he said, looking down at the broken toy and picking it up. "Amanda, is this yours?"

"Yes, Mr. Penn," she said timidly. She wanted to cry, but if she cried in front of Briton, he wouldn't forget and would taunt her for the rest of her life.

"You should be more careful with your toys. You know, I don't mind it, but toys aren't generally allowed. We don't want you to lose them."

"He broke Violet Red's face," she said, glaring at Briton.

"So that's why there's no right eye," the monitor said to himself, looking the toy over.

He looked over at the boy trying to feign surprise. "Briton, what do you have to say for yourself?"

"It wasn't my fault, Mr. Penn! It fell off! The thing's eyes are practically ready to fall off!"

"He's lying!" one of the girls said. "I saw him pull it off. I swear!"

"And then he stomped on it!" another girl cried out.

"And then he peed on it!" a boy called out from somewhere Amanda couldn't see.

Amanda rolled her eyes, but it was kinda funny. She found herself laughing at the remark and the immaturity of the unknown kid.

"Okay, okay, Mr. Clown," he said, looking over at a boy who was watching the scene from a few feet away. "I don't smell any urine."

"I didn't do anything," Briton said, hurriedly.

"You have two girls and a class clown who say otherwise," Taylor said, frowning and holding the dog in his hands carefully. Taylor was a tough guy, but he had a heart for Amanda at least. "You're coming with me. I don't know why…"

Amanda couldn't hear what Taylor didn't know as the two walked into the school. Recess was over.

THE FEELING OF being left without her best friend pinched and prodded at her. Taylor still had the toy with him. She felt lost without Violet Red. Not only was he the recess monitor, but he also did duty as one of the school janitors.

She couldn't focus at all on the history lesson. Occasionally, she caught things like "civil war," and something called "abolish" but she couldn't focus.

She kept obsessing over what Taylor was doing with her dog. She hoped that the toy was sitting in Lost and Found, waiting for her to come pick her up. Even though she was broken and bruised, she still loved Violet Red.

"I miss you," she murmured to herself.

"Amanda," Miss Hammett said sternly. She looked up at her. "Are you with us?"

Amanda murmured a yes.

"Okay. Can you tell us who was President during the time of the Civil War?" she asked skeptically.

"Lincoln Logs?" Amanda asked.

A commotion of laughter erupted from the room. She felt her face redden in embarrassment.

It was a bit shocking to see that even Miss Hammett was laughing. "I'll give you credit for that, Amanda. Yes. It was Abraham Lincoln. Lincoln Logs, by the way, actually came about many years later, in the 1920s. Just in case anyone was curious," she said, a small smile on her face.

"Did you play with Lincoln Logs, Miss Hammett?" Briton asked innocently. Amanda wanted to walk over to him and punch him in the face.

Or, even better, cut his legs off his stupid, boyish body. She relished in that murderous fantasy.

"I did, Briton," Miss Hammett said. "But right now we're focused on learning about the Civil—"

"Legos are better," he interrupted. A few kids snorted at Briton's remark.

"Oh, really?" questioned Miss Hammett, smirking.

What was going on? Miss Hammett was not normally like this!

"Yeah! Like, they snap in place, and you can build rocket ships!" quipped Dexter, getting riled up as usual when his brother rarely got the teacher distracted.

Miss Hammett smiled as she walked over to the cabinet where she kept the good toys and pulled out a set of Lincoln Logs.

"And you can build houses and dungeons and lots of other cool things!" another kid called out.

"You know what?" Miss Hammett said as she brought two sets to a large table in front of everyone. "I think we need to have some fun today. Everyone, gather around!"

Obediently, everyone got up from their seat, except for Briton. He scowled as the teacher reprimanded him, and he ambled over to the large table.

"All right, kids," she said, clapping her hands together. Miss Hammett certainly *was* in a good mood! "Let's work together and build a cabin!"

Just as Amanda had settled down, she saw Taylor open the door to the classroom, smiling.

"Hey Miss Hammett," he said, walking over to the table. "Would it be all right to borrow Amanda—"

He looked at the table. "Lincoln Logs! I haven't played with those since I was a kid!"

"We're learning about Lincoln," one of the kids said, holding a few of the logs in his hands.

"What better way to learn about Abraham Lincoln," he said. Turning to Miss Hammett, he whispered something Amanda could barely make out. She saw her teacher slightly grin and reply something, which made Taylor laugh.

"Amanda, you may leave with Mr. Penn," she said, going back to her toys.

"It won't be long, I promise," assured Taylor as they walked out of the room.

Taylor led her down the hall and into the principal's office. She wasn't sure why Taylor was bringing her there, but when she entered the room and saw her toy again, she could feel her heartbeat's drum-like nature beat against her skin in excitement.

"Violet Red!" she squealed, running over to the principal's desk and grabbing it quickly, clutching it.

She looked at its face and saw that someone had sewed the eye back on, and it looked like it was when she first got it.

"Amanda Toms," the principal said, smiling down at her. "Can you tell me what happened today during recess?"

Amanda told everything that happened to Principal Stone. He listened with rapt attention and shook his head in disappointment.

"I know you're very happy to have your toy back," he said to her, looking up at Taylor. "And I've dealt with Mr. Briton personally." Principal Stone took a really good look at the toy and smiled again. "That's quite the toy you've got there, you know."

"I love Violet Red," she blurted out.

"That's a very beautiful name, Amanda," Principal Stone said. "Can I tell you something?"

Amanda nodded.

"Taylor fixed Violet Red up for you. You should be very lucky that he had the tools needed for the job."

Amanda turned to Taylor right before the principal was about to ask her to thank him. She got up from the chair and hugged him tight. "Thank you for making Violet Red feel better! Thank you so much! She looks just like she did when I first got her for Christmas!"

"It was nothing," Taylor replied, his ears going red from embarrassment.

"Violet Red says you're the best doctor ever!"

"Does she now?"

"She's very happy!"

Principal Stone looked very pleased. He looked over at Taylor. "Now you know what it's like when the students appreciate us."

"Does this mean I'll get a raise?" joked Taylor.

"In your dreams," he quipped back before having Taylor walk her back to the classroom.

THE REST OF the school day was better than the first few hours. Amanda clung to Violet Red even more than she ever had – she was not going to risk another situation with Briton or his brother. She did not want to risk another situation with anyone, not even her teacher.

Her mother asked her about her day, and Amanda was quick to say everything that happened. Terri wasn't very thrilled with hearing about what Briton did with the toy and she thought that it would be a good idea to talk to his parents. She made a mental note on the way home to talk to them after suppertime. When they walked in the door, they were greeted by the smells of chicken and rice cooking. Terri could feel her stomach rumbling.

"That smells amazing," she said as she entered the kitchen. Seeing a couple small pots cooking on the stove, she noticed green beans, rice, and gravy cooking. She began to salivate at the sights and the smells before her.

"And it will be ready in about five minutes," replied Delana, taking a sip of her white wine.

"Five minutes too long," remarked Terri, taking a small bite of the gravy, nearly burning her tongue. "I'm guessing dessert is cooling in the fridge?"

Delana opened the door to the fridge, revealing what looked like a cheesecake. "I didn't make it," she explained. "I bought a strawberry cheesecake from that bakery you love."

"One of these days, I hope to marry you," Terri said, grinning. Walking over, she embraced Delana and kissed her. She giggled as she returned the kiss, walking back to the pots and seasoning the food.

"Cheesecake always makes you want to marry me."

"It does something else to me."

Delana laughed as she turned the heat down on the stove. "Our first official date," she remarked.

"Involved a cheesecake," Terri finished, tempted to open the fridge door and take a small bite of the dessert calling out to her.

"In bed."

"Naked."

The women turned to each other, their eyes flaring in arousal. Moments like this made the both of them happy that they made the decision to live together.

Delana gave Terri a look that told her it was time to set the table. As she was pulling plates out of the cabinet, she heard somebody scream from outside. At first, she didn't piece together it was coming from the house across the street.

It was as though the scream was intensified by a thousand percent. It pierced the romantic atmosphere built up by cheesecake and genuine love, frightening the women about to sit down for a hot meal. Abandoning the comfort and scents of the kitchen, Delana and Terri rushed out of the house and doubled back.

One of the boys was lying down on the ground, a pool of blood infusing into snow. Terri was too scared to move – she was frozen in place, like a snowman – but Delana was the brave one, slowly approaching a very distraught neighbor.

"My God," Delana whispered as she saw the little unconscious boy. "My God. What happened?"

Belinda was close to inconsolable. She could hardly speak. She could barely even stutter. She kept pointing at her son, whispering his name.

Then she screamed again. But this time, she could articulate his name. It was as though the women were listening to a horrific broken record.

Terri turned to the boy's brother. "Dexter, right?" She didn't wait for a response. "Run into the house and call 911, would you?"

It was almost surprising how something so traumatic hardly touched her soul. A boy was unconscious. *A child was attacked.* And all she could hear was a calm voice telling a child to call 911 for an ambulance! She wasn't sure if she should be disgusted at herself, or if she should be proud for not freaking out. But a selfish part of her was grateful that the child in the snow was not hers. At least Amanda was not the one who was severely harmed. She almost had to slap herself across the face for not exhibiting much empathy for the upset mother barely seven feet away from her.

Both Delana and Terri wanted to stick by their neighbor to find out what happened to Briton. They decided against it, despite the curiosity. As they turned to walk back to their home, they noticed a little girl that wasn't theirs, looking out the living room window and smiling. They continued to stare at this African American child, giving a smile that indicated it was celebrating a perverted victory. It brought chills down

Terri's spine.. She turned her head to tell Delana something, but when she looked back, the little girl was gone.

She was gone in the blink of an eye.

-11-

It was difficult for Terri to let her child out of her sight, especially after what had happened to Briton. She wasn't exactly sure what occurred, but there was somebody in her neighborhood who wasn't exactly kind towards children. She hadn't bothered to connect with Belinda after the unfortunate accident, but Terri was more than grateful, more than happy for Belinda, to see them walking back inside the house after being gone for five days. She had to restrain herself more than usual to keep herself from going over there and asking Belinda to spill everything. She finally came to the conclusion that the neighborhood wasn't exactly the safest place in Grand Rapids, let alone Michigan. No matter the cause of the event, the realization that not even a child was safe in her quiet neighborhood seized her with such tempestuous fear she nearly considered moving.

It's just one isolated event. Nothing has happened since.

It's only been five days.

That horrid person is lurking in the shadows, waiting for Amanda to come out of the house unguarded.

There was a slight feeling of comfort knowing that Jeff was no longer the prime suspect in Ida's murder. The evening news brought her some solace in knowing whoever killed Jeff's wife was in jail, but it also alarmed her to know that this man was responsible for the kidnapping and possible murder of a woman and her child.

But despite knowing that the man who had killed Ida and possibly this woman named Lynnette Redd, it brought her a sense of consternation that this woman's child, that this potentially deceased little girl, had a familiar name.

Her name was Violet Redd.

She became even more curious about this case and became even more interested and involved in the evening news over the next few days. She was tempted to give Detective Ian a call and learn more about what was going on in the case of Lynnette and Violet Redd. But they probably would not be akin to divulging any details. But she did learn, of her own accord, the two were killed.

The little girl was African American and was Amanda's age. They were found in Biff Harder's basement, lying side by side. Biff Harder was the murderer. It was never Jeff. It was this evil man who had killed these people, who was also tied to Ida's death.

Knowing that her daughter had this little girl's most recent toy made her want to gag. In fact, she did heave in the toilet when she first heard the little girl's name. She had to get that toy away from Amanda. She had to!

Unfortunately, she had little opportunity to do so, and after a couple days, immediately knew that there would be no way to get it away from her. Ridiculous, she told herself. It's ridiculous that I can't be assertive enough to take the toy away.

And then an opportunity presented itself.

Terri took a glance at the living room clock. It was about fifteen minutes before she had to drop her daughter off at school. She got up from the couch and walked to Amanda's door, lightly knocking.

"Amanda!" she called out. "We need to get going."

She opened the door and noticed Amanda was petting the toy and talking to it. Amanda looked up and frowned at her mother. Her eyes seemed rather sunken. She looked upset.

"Is there something wrong, honey?" asked Terri.

Amanda didn't respond.

Terri took a nervous step closer to her daughter and said her name again. She reached out her hand to touch Amanda's shoulder.

A voice unfamiliar to Terri thundered from Amanda. In a peculiar, distorted voice, she shrieked, "DON'T FUCKING TOUCH ME YOU DYKE!"

Terri swore and jumped back in terror.

It wasn't her daughter sitting on the bed. Whatever was seated at the base of the mattress, on top of a cartoonish comforter, was something she would have seen in a horror movie. Whatever was sitting there had a contorted, diseased face. The creature in the room laughed at her as Terri scrambled out.

Running out of the hallway, she steered herself in the kitchen. She knew Delana was there. She needed her comfort!

But she wasn't there.

An African American woman taller than Delana stood, her back facing Terri. She slowly turned herself around. The woman standing before her had beautiful long hair, but the face covered by the hair was far from beautiful. There were deep scars all over her face. Her eyes were also sunken. In a low voice, she spoke to Terri. "We ain't here for you," it said rather roughly.

Terri stammered as she asked who she was here for.

But she didn't get a response. The voice of someone else cut through the terror, crying out her name.

THE HARSH FEELING of being slapped took Terri by surprise. She found herself in bed, trembling and in a cold sweat.

"Terri!" cried Delana, relieved that Terri was out of her

night terror. "My God! I was so close to calling an ambulance!"

Terri attempted to sit up. Delana carefully grabbed her by the arms and slowly pulled her in a sitting position. "Wh-what happened?" she stammered.

"I brought Amanda to school. You overslept. You looked so calm, but then I got home, and I saw you shaking and screaming. It was terrifying," answered Delana.

Without any hesitation or any prompting, Terri explained everything she had dreamt. It was almost surreal in that she could never remember her dreams, but this one was beyond anything she had ever experienced. She almost began trembling again as she found herself vacuumed back into that horror.

Delana was silent for a few minutes. She coughed and placed a hand on her partner's leg. "You dreamt about the murdered woman and her child? They didn't release any pictures of them; at least, to my knowledge, they didn't."

"There's something odd going on," murmured Terri. "Delana, the little girl's name is Violet Redd."

"Amanda must have heard it somewhere," replied Delana.

"Where? At school?"

"Possibly?"

"It must have been at school. I think we should ask administration, if they're able to divulge at least a name."

"You're going to drive up to the school, walk into the offices, and ask, 'did a little girl by the name of Violet Redd attend this school?' Come on, Terri. That's kinda weird, even for you."

Terri found herself on the defensive. "I'm not saying that she might have attended."

"So you think Amanda overheard the name, either from other kids or teachers?"

"Maybe? Or maybe you've got something with this dead girl attending Amanda's school," Terri replied, now considering the theory Violet Redd could have walked the same halls as Amanda. She now toyed with the idea that Violet Redd swung on the same swing, went down the same plastic slide that her daughter did at recess.

"You're coming with," Terri said, rising from the bed.

Delana couldn't help but laugh. "Don't you think that you could wait until school lets out?"

Terri found herself grinning as well. "Right, of course. I can wait."

AMANDA LOATHED DELANA as she drove her to the school. Delana had seen her place the toy in her bag and tried to stop her. Amanda threw a fit. Not only was the minor disruption to the norm frustrating, but that bitch didn't want her bringing toys to school.

She could feel her irritation lessen as she left Delana's car and ran to the entrance of the school. As soon as she got inside, she pulled Violet Red out of the bag.

"I won't let anyone hurt you," Violet Red said to Amanda.

"Thanks. You're my only friend," she said back.

Nobody heard her. She ignored the kids around her and headed to her classroom. The teacher was distracted with one of the other students, so Amanda placed Violet Red on the desk and pulled out her things from her bag.

"I won't let that bitch hurt you," Violet Red said.

"She's mean," whispered Amanda in agreement.

Violet Red repeated herself. Amanda found herself smiling. She had been hearing a little girl speak to her for a while now. At first, she assumed she was dreaming. But now it was just a normal part of Amanda's reality. It sounded just like that little girl she met at her dad's house. When she heard the voice for the first time say that Ida would no longer hurt her again, she was relieved.

And as much as Amanda would have been ashamed to admit, she was actually *thrilled* when she heard Ida was dead.

She would have loved to go to that horrible woman's funeral and spit on her face.

Violet Red wanted nothing more than to be loved and held by a child. And it would do the same thing for her. She would protect Amanda for as long as Amanda was still loving her and caring for her. Violet Red said that there was another child before her, but Violet Red never had the chance to really connect with that child. It was stolen from her. And Violet Red vowed that it would love and protect a child from the harm that had befallen its previous owner.

"Amanda! I told you, no toys on your desk during lessons!" Miss Hammett cried out sternly. Before Amanda could say anything, she snatched the toy by its paw.

Miss Hammett yelped as a sharp pain pinched her finger, where she had gripped the ribbon. In a jerk reaction, she threw the toy on her desk.

Amanda whimpered. Then, to her surprise, she felt her mouth change shape. "You shouldn't have done that," she smirked.

Miss Hammett leered at Amanda. "Why not?"

Amanda didn't respond. But she could hear Violet Red say quite clearly, "She shouldn't have done that."

ABOUT THE TIME that the bell would ring for lunch, an announcement came over the school speakers. Principal Stone made a brief announcement, stating that outside recess was cancelled; instead, one of the gym teachers brought out the good games for the kids to play instead of just hanging around, waiting to go back to class.

Ginger looked at the paperwork on her desk after cleaning up the art supplies left by the kids before they left for lunch. She hated doing anything with art, but she knew the kids enjoyed it. She knew that messing around with crayons and markers and paintbrushes got them to be active in their learning – which she didn't mind – but the cleanup was hell.

Muttering under her breath, she shoved the remaining crayon boxes back on the light green shelf a few feet away from her desk. As she sat at her desk, her eyes fell on a picture of her and her daughter.

She was only eight years old when her life was taken from her. The pool accident two years ago invaded her mind, like a bug found crawling on the wall, practically asking for its untimely death. She put a flyswatter to that memory and wondered if the love she had for these kids was now amplified since Charlotte's death. Charlotte was her baby, her only child.

It's unfortunate that a child's death could cause such a domino effect on the rest of her life, personally and professionally. When the domino of death fell, it ended almost everything, save for her teaching career. At the time, she was wrapping up her graduate degree and was ready to marry the man she loved for nine years.

The grief impacted her and Taylor differently. He resorted to working in the garage, while she made continuous poor decisions affecting their intimate unity. When he found out, he packed up all his stuff and moved out. The distance made them realize that marriage was not for them, but they still had something there. They decided to remain friends, almost working alongside one another.

She didn't realize she had put that stuffed dog next to the picture. She wanted to pick that thing up and admire it, but the memory of that sharp pain came back to her. She grabbed it from the nape of its neck, caressing it. A slight lavender smell emanated from the toy. There was another scent on the toy, one she couldn't place. A faint smell of burning cloth was also present.

Odd, she thought.

The sound of someone humming made her jump out of the chair. She could hear the sound of a young child murmuring a melody, but it was so distant and muffled she wondered if maybe one of her kids was heading back to the classroom. She got up and opened the door.

There was nobody there.

She closed the door and walked back to her seat. As soon as she sat down, the humming came back, but it was slightly louder than it was before. It sounded like it was coming from somewhere inside the classroom, but she knew she was the only one there.

In all the time she used this classroom, she never had problems with the closet door. She hardly used the closet unless she needed the projector, which was about once a month.

It was slowly opening on its own.

The humming was now gone, but in its place was a song so disturbing she thought it could only come from the mind of a Gothic poet.

Two little girls, dressed in red.
One girl alive, the other one dead.
Don't close your eyes, don't rest your head.
She is watching – the dead girl in red.

"No," Ginger croaked as she saw a little black girl appear before her eyes, holding scissors in her hands, walking over to her. As the girl drew nearer, Ginger's lips parted as she realized there was something not quite right about what she was seeing: the little girl was transparent, but the more she moved, the less transparent she became. She became more solid at each ghostly step.

She got up and ran for the door.

It wouldn't open.

The lament picked back up again as she scrambled back to her desk in terror. Ginger wanted nothing more than to defend herself. Her mind immediately attempted to rationalize killing a child, but how could you kill something that wasn't even alive? How could you kill something that seemed to be not from this world?

"You didn't jump in the pool," said this little girl very crudely. "You didn't bother to save your daughter."

Ginger attempted to defend the words hurled at her with stuttering, incoherent excuses. The little girl laughed. Suddenly, the name Violet Redd appeared in her mind.

Wasn't that the name of the toy sitting accusingly at her desk?

"You were too busy fucking that hippie," the girl continued. "You're a whore, Ginger Trudy Hammett."

"I'M NOT A WHORE!" Ginger screamed. Surely someone would hear her, would come and rescue her.

"Was his dick bigger than mine?" she heard Taylor say. But he wasn't there. His voice was coming out of the little girl's childish mouth. "Did he pleasure you better than I ever did? Was the pleasure better than when we conceived the daughter you murdered?"

"GET AWAY FROM ME!" she yelled.

Nobody was coming in to save her. She had to act. And fast!

She felt something sharp against her ankle and she fell. She hastily turned herself around, facing the little girl who now had a face only known to Dante and Virgil. There was no longer a little girl standing over her. It had changed its face and whatever this demon spawn was called was now grinning maniacally, scissors above its head. Ginger scrambled backwards, away from the demon.

The way that thing ambled over to Ginger made it seem as though she was playing a game she wanted nothing to do with – a sick game of Life. If this thing really wanted to kill her, it would have done so by now. She held on to the leg of one of the desks and attempted to stand, but the pain was so unbearable she couldn't get herself to get up from her position on the floor.

The little girl was gone.

She let out a sigh of relief as she slowly got up.

But she fell down.

And the little girl was back, not just holding the scissors, but one hand was now clutching onto the ribboned paw of the dog and the other hand poised to stab her.

There was no time to scream. The little girl plunged the sharp scissors deep into her neck, then again.

And again.

Blood sputtered out of her mouth and neck, staining the chair, the desk, the toy the girl was clutching. She reached a hand to her mouth, but she wasn't able to do so without shaking and causing more blood stains on the floor of her classroom.

Then the girl stabbed her right in the heart.

Her sight became blurrier at each stab. All she saw was the door to her room open. All she heard was the horrified screams as her students watched their teacher's life being stolen from them.

-12-

In all the years Mickey had been on the police force, he had never walked into such a gruesome, grotesque scene like the one he walked into when he entered Ginger Hammett's classroom. Even though Ian was not there with him, he did have several other officers with him as he inspected the room. Whoever had killed this poor educator could still be on school property, hence the reason why a large number of officers were patrolling the grounds. All the little kids were ushered out of the school, their parents notified. He couldn't help but feel sorry for administration, who would have to deal with angry, concerned parents calling in fear for the safety of their children.

He couldn't blame them.

He also wanted to vomit.

Mickey had never seen so much blood before. It was on the floor. It was on the desks. There wasn't a spot in the room that didn't have blood. He looked over at one of the officers with him. The young woman was clearly shaken by the scene before her eyes. She pushed her long, red hair away from her eyes and looked at Mickey.

"Holy shit," she said.

"There's nothing holy about this," said Mickey, his voice lowered.

"The killer had to have been crawling on the floor, to make sure the teacher was subdued enough so he could stab her in the neck and chest. That's why the killer went for the dorsalis pedis artery."

Mickey watched the female officer in amazement. "How do you know all this?"

"Med school," she said, her eyes still on the crime scene. "Wanted to be a doctor but decided to join the police force."

"So the killer subdues her," said Mickey, going back to business, "Then either he or she—"

Andrea forced back a laugh. "It's a man that did this, not a woman."

"And what makes you believe this was the work of a man?"

"Oh, come on," scolded Andrea. "The number of women killers can't hold a candle to the number of male killers in this country, let alone the world."

"But that doesn't mean—"

"She's too weak to attempt to stand," she interrupted. "She scrambles back. I'm guessing there is a struggle to attempt to stand."

"Then the killer begins acting as though she's a grilled steak or a Caesar salad."

Andrea's eyes narrowed, her gaze cold and stiff. "That isn't appropriate."

"Is this the appropriate time to criticize how I'd explain the murder to a layperson?" Mickey countered.

"I just didn't—"

"I know you don't like Ian because of what you call his 'Frat boy personality,' but the boy at least knows how to handle himself. It makes this job a lot easier to handle, especially…"

Mickey didn't bother to put the rest of the sentence into words; instead, he gestured his hands dramatically around the room. "These things hardly happen here. This is probably one of the worst murders our town has ever dealt with. Ian?

Yeah, he's got his way of doing things, but that's because we aren't used to this kind of thing here."

Andrea didn't say anything. She watched Mickey as he continued the crime scene investigation. "I think he should be put on desk duty," she muttered.

Mickey heard what she said. Furiously, he dropped something and stared at her.

"That would be of severe detriment to not just him, but the department," he snapped.

"He couldn't handle this, and you damn well know it," Andrea said coolly.

"If it wasn't for him, we wouldn't have caught the man who killed the Redd's."

"I heard what he did," Andrea said, a frustrated small smile slowly making its way on her pale complexion. "He offered the man food. He practically forced the man to confess. You treat a criminal the way they should be treated – like a criminal, not a friend!"

"The man was homeless!" Mickey shouted, not caring that others were making their way into the room.

"Hey, what's going on?" one of the officers asked.

"Nothing," Andrea answered curtly.

"Larry, come here for a second, would you?" Mickey gestured for the officer to come over to them.

"What's up?"

"What do you think about Ian?" asked Mickey, his eyes fixated on Andrea's. "Andrea thinks he should be on desk duty."

Bemused, Larry covered his mouth as he coughed. "Ian? I think he's one of the best. We wouldn't have made so much progress over the last couple of years if he was on desk duty." He laughed. "The guy's people skills are—"

"Inappropriate for this work," Andrea cut in.

"Woah there," Larry said, staring Andrea down.

"What is wrong with this department?" cried Andrea. "I've done this work for five years, and I've never seen this level of incompetence."

"Excuse me?" snickered Mickey. "You're joking, right? You practically need people skills for this work!"

"Yes, but to a point. Ian's level of people skills are more appropriate for a counselor or a psychologist. Not for a detective who has to remain distant from the people he interacts with. End of discussion."

She finished up the investigation without interruption from the men who had been working for the department longer than she'd been there. As they packed up their things and everyone else was done, she turned to Mickey. "I'll be reporting all this incompetence to the head, just so you know. Ian will be on desk duty, and you will be, too, if you continue allowing Ian to make unethical choices."

Mickey sighed. As tempted as he was to counteract her stupid argument, he remained silent as he took a couple of the evidence bags. As he walked out of the school, he placed the things securely in the Grand Rapids Police Department car and closed the door.

A voice spoke out, but not one that could be heard with typical ears. The stuffed dog sitting in the car whimpered out a faint sound.

"Amanda," whispered Violet Red. "I'm coming home."

IT HAD BEEN a long, excruciating day. Most of the stress was due to the murder of Ginger Hammett, but Mickey was done with the day after going back to the precinct and took care of a few other things. All he wanted to do was go home, pour himself a large whiskey coke, and settle in his couch and watch TV for a few hours, and maybe pick up some Chinese food.

That sounds like perfection, he thought to himself as he drove himself to the Chinese restaurant to pick up his order.

He pulled into the parking lot and walked inside. The smell of fried rice and egg rolls filled up the place, causing his stomach to rumble. Placing a hand on his stomach, he walked to the counter, where a young man was situated, arguing with someone. The young man looked up at Mickey as though he was pleading for mercy.

"…burnt wontons! You serve this to your children?" the man in front of him shouted, thrusting the bag of food in front of the cashier's face.

"Please, leave," the young man cried. "You're making our customers uncomfortable. Please!"

"I'm making them uncomfortable?" The man laughed scornfully and took the bag, throwing a fat hand inside and pulling out what looked like an egg roll. Before he could do whatever he had planned, Mickey grabbed the overweight "gentleman" by the shoulder.

The man spun around fast and dropped the egg roll before his fist attempted to make contact with Mickey's face. Surprised, Mickey grabbed him by the wrist and squeezed. Hard.

"You leave this restaurant, now, or I'll throw you in custody for not just assaulting an officer, but assaulting a waiter, d'you hear me?" hissed Mickey.

"Fuck you, pig," the customer replied. Mickey could smell the alcohol on this man's breath and reconsidered drinking tonight.

"Let's go," he ordered.

"No," the man responded.

Mickey unhooked his handcuffs. "You're under arrest for—"

Something sharp hit him in the back. He took a quick breath and turned around. Just as he was reaching for his gun, the drunken man held a knife to the back of Mickey's neck. He kicked behind him to get the drunk man off his back. He stumbled just as Mickey turned around and pointed the gun at him. It seemed that everyone in the restaurant was watching the scene, as though it was a train wreck before their eyes.

The man dropped his knife. Mickey acted fast and threw him in the back of the car. As he was about to pull out of the driveway, the young man at the counter ran out the door, holding a bag of greasy Chinese food.

"On the house!" he exclaimed.

"What?" Mickey cried out, looking at the man who was handing him his bag of sesame chicken and fried rice. "Also threw in a few of those donuts and an extra egg roll for you. It's our way of thanking you for removing that drunk ass from the restaurant."

Mickey thanked the man and drove off, ready to put this man away for assault. The smell of the hot food was taunting him as they drove off. He was tempted to pull out an egg roll and harass the drunkard with hot food but thought better of it.

Better not be unprofessional, or Andrea will put me on desk duty, he thought to himself, smirking.

"What were you thinking?" Mickey asked as they were six blocks away, looking at his backseat passenger through the rearview mirror.

But the man was snoring.

Mickey shook his head and took out an egg roll.

He didn't see the little black girl standing in the middle of the road, holding a bloody toy in her arms.

Looking up, Mickey swore and swerved. He stopped the car and looked around for the girl, but she wasn't there anymore. He looked at the back of the police car, and to his amazement, the drunk guy was gone! He looked frantically around – he couldn't have gotten very far.

"I'm going crazy," he said to himself as he went back to the car, focusing on finding his missing assailant. He was about to put it back into drive, but then he felt something sharp pressed against his arm.

A cut was forming on his wrist.

And it was growing bigger by the minute.

"Shit!" Mickey exclaimed. Suddenly, something slammed

his head against the wheel. Whatever was holding his head violently thrusted it against the glass which separated the criminals from the officer. He looked back through the rearview mirror. To his relief, the man was back, but the glass was locked in place. There was no way he could've reached out and grabbed him. There was no way it could've happened. It wasn't possible!

How the fuck was that possible?

He reached for his gun as he screamed for whatever it was to get off him.

Whatever was assaulting him had let go and Mickey took a few deep breaths in and out. He had his gun in his hand and looked around. There was no way the drunk man could have done that.

It made no sense.

After a few minutes, Mickey was calm enough to get back on the road. As he placed his hands back on the wheel, he looked down at his wrist.

The cut was gone.

HE CHOSE NOT to tell anyone about what had just happened when he got back to the precinct and booked the drunk man. The man didn't have a record and was just acting out. It was odd behavior, but sometimes people do peculiar things without any rhyme or reason. As soon as he was done with everything he needed to do, he left for the day, his Chinese food slowly going cold in the passenger seat of his car.

It was almost six o'clock when he arrived home. He sat the food on the counter and immediately went to the fridge, pulling out a can of Coke and the bottle of whiskey from the counter next to the fridge. He opened the bottle and took a whiff of the alcohol. It was a strange habit, but he loved the smell of alcohol, when it wasn't on someone else's breath, at least.

Mickey grabbed a large glass from the cabinet and opened the soda, pouring both the alcohol and the soda at the same time. When he was satisfied with the amount of liquid in the cup, he took a sip and let out a sigh of relief and pleasure. He wasn't a heavy drinker, but he did like to wind down with at least two drinks before turning away for the evening.

The sound of something moving around sparked his attention as he sat his glass down and turned around.

There was nothing there.

"You're losing it," he said out loud and picked up the drink again, taking another large sip. His back facing the bag of Chinese food, he reached for a plate.

Once again, he heard the same noise. Something trying to get out of a paper bag; something dumb enough to think the butt-end was the escape route. It made him drop his plate. He turned around fast and *saw the bag moving slowly from the counter.*

His eyes growing as wide as they possibly could, he reached his arm out and slowly grabbed the bag.

It stopped moving.

Furiously, Mickey took out the contents of the bag – a large white container of food and a small bag of egg rolls were in there.

Nothing else besides food.

He shook his head and pulled out a fork from the drawer underneath. He took everything into the living room, sat it down on the glass coffee table and grabbed the remote, turning the television on.

As soon as he found something to watch, he began to eat.

"Stuffing your face again, are we, Mickey?" a voice said in his ear.

He almost choked on a piece of chicken and turned his head to face whoever had invaded his privacy.

There wasn't anybody there. The room's temperature dropped. Mickey could almost see his breath.

"Food won't keep you safe like I can," the voice said.

"Who's there?" cried Mickey.

No response.

He knew that voice. It was his mother. God rest her soul. She passed away five years ago. He hadn't heard her voice for a long time.

There was nothing anybody could have done for her. Not him. Not his sister. She was alone and vulnerable, and the nursing home knew it.

But they hired the wrong person for the job. A complete failing on the part of the home, they hired a man who should not have been around the elderly. The man robbed at least four other people before he robbed Robin, his mother. He didn't know a whole lot about what happened – all he knew was that she woke up after hearing the thief go through her personal belongings, and he stabbed her with a lethal dosage of her medication.

She was killed within an hour.

And nobody cared.

"Save some of that for later," the voice said to him. "Don't eat the whole damn thing. You'll get fat."

He turned around and saw his mother, sitting there on the couch.

"Mommy," he whimpered.

"You left me there, Mickey. You left me there to die."

"You were sick, Mommy. There was nothing we could've done. We didn't have—"

"You lie to your mother? How can you do something like that? You shame me and your father."

"Mommy, I'm—"

"Sorry? You're not sorry."

He looked away, turned his head away. He couldn't face her.

"This isn't real," he said aloud. He turned around.

It wasn't his mother, but the little girl who he thought was standing in the middle of the road was there. She had the fork in one hand, the stuffed dog in the other. He winced – the blood was still on the toy and the color looked darker than it did when he bagged it and recorded it as evidence.

Before he could do anything, she lunged at him, stabbing him in the eyes. Mickey screamed. He got up, but something pulled him down to the ground.

"You shouldn't have left your mother to die," the little girl hissed at him. She sunk the fork deep into his face and pulled down.

"You shouldn't have taken me away from my friend, either," the girl said as she reached for the gun on the coffee table. Mickey reached an arm out to grab her but failed. She shoved the barrel of the gun into Mickey's mouth, then forced Mickey's hand to take the gun by the grip. He wanted to fight her, but the supernatural strength of this child was too much for him to handle.

Her fingers curled around Mickey's finger on the trigger, and she pressed down.

Nothing.

Mickey laughed as he attempted to release himself from the grip of this demonic child. "You think you're gonna kill me? A seasoned det—"

-13-

News of Detective Mickey Adams' murder spread across the whole nation. On every major news outlet, there was coverage of the brutal, macabre murder of the detective. Terri couldn't peel her eyes away from her television. She had the radio tuned into the news as she worked at the store. She did not want to miss a thing. It infuriated Delana to the point where she removed the radio from the kitchen. Terri hardly knew the man. Yet, there was an intense curiosity, an obsessive need, to make sure she was kept informed of the entire situation. She wanted whoever killed Mickey held responsible, wanted them to suffer the second they were caught.

But another situation demanded her attention, even more than the chaos of a local detective murdered. Her daughter had become so inconsolable after the death of her teacher that she had to pull her out of school for an unknown amount of time. She did more than just throw fits – she became violent. The other evening as Delana was gathering up Amanda's clothes, Amanda came rushing out of her closet and nearly clocked her with a baseball bat. Terri had no idea where she got the bat, but she yanked it out of her hands, hastily grabbed the clothes bin and Delana by the hand and dragged them out of Amanda's room. She went to the hardware store and bought a lock. As much as it pained Terri to do so, she had to ensure the safety of everyone. It meant going into Amanda's room while she was at her father's house and removing anything that could possibly be seen as a potential weapon against anyone, especially Amanda.

When she made the retreat into Amanda's bedroom, she was horrified to discover all of her stuffed animals were ripped. It had to have been recent – they were all in one piece just the other night. She took the time to pick up all the stuffing and threw them in the garbage. She did a deep clean of Amanda's room. She did everything she could humanly do to ensure that this room was safe for her daughter.

Then there was a very frightening run-in with a carpet cleaner. Terri had no idea what she was doing when it came to deep cleaning, so she hired a young man named Brent to do the work. Amanda happened to be in her room at the time. When Terri asked her daughter to come out of her room so that he could work, she threw another temper tantrum. She called her mother a very nasty word. Terri came close to slapping her daughter, but instead dragged her away, Amanda still screaming. Terri, uncomfortable by the whole moment, did her best to act as though everything was okay.

About ten minutes later, there was a close call between Brent and Amanda. He was about to begin working in the closet when Amanda snuck behind him, a knife in hand. She almost bolted right into him, but had Delana not been where she was, that poor young man would've been seriously injured. Terri watched, frozen in place, as Delana grabbed Amanda from behind and finagled her way to get the knife out of her grasp. Brent should have freaked out and left the house, but he didn't.

He should have pressed charges.

He took his time before he finally left. Brent looked at Terri, confused but also worried as he put his things back into his car. "I hope your daughter gets some help. Man, that was some freaky shit," he said as he closed the trunk.

Terri looked at the car, not wanting to make eye contact with the young man. "She sees a doctor. Again, I'm so sorry for what happened earlier."

He shrugged. "If it were me, I'd put my daughter safe in a hospital, where she couldn't cause any more harm. But whatever. I'm not hurt. Just shocked."

That should've been the last straw. But in Terri's dangerous, deluded mind, all Amanda needed was a routine checkup. She took her daughter in to the doctor's office, about two days later. But as she drove Amanda to the doctor's office, she knew she was only fooling herself.

You have to say something, she thought as she pulled into the parking lot of the hospital with her daughter.

She sat in the waiting room, nervously scratching her arm. She relayed all the horrible things that had happened recently to the doctor. They said they probably won't have answers for what was happening but assumed that it was very likely there was some kind of psychotic break. It was probably something called Oppositional Defiant Disorder, according to Dr. Sperling. They wanted to make sure it wasn't anything biological before they could make any final conclusion, which meant Terri would have to look for a child psychologist. She practically fainted, thinking about all the bills that would come in the mail.

"Terri Connors," said one of the nurses at the hospital. It wasn't a question. She stood up from her chair really fast, nearly falling back into it. She followed the nurse into one of the rooms. She wondered where Amanda was.

Terri asked immediately as she took a seat in the doctor's office, "What's wrong with my daughter?"

Dr. Sperling stared at Terri for a moment before clearing his throat. "Has your daughter ever seen the horror film, or read the book, *The Exorcist*?"

"What? No. I don't let my daughter near horror films, let alone scary books. She's too young for that."

"Well, there's a scene in the film – I think it's also in the book – where Reagan attacks the nurses and verbally accosts the doctor. Ms. Connors, I'll be frank with you. There's nothing physically wrong with your daughter. I do think she needs to be seen by someone who's more qualified than I am to handle this situation."

"A child psychologist?" asked Terri, very weakly. "We can't afford to do that. One of them looked her over, and she even admitted it was out of her purview! Christ! I'm still paying her!"

The doctor looked at her pitifully. It made Terri want to punch the guy. "She needs to be tended to. In my professional opinion, it is not safe for your daughter to live with you and your… erm, significant other… or even your ex-husband."

"So you want her to be locked up in some mental asylum?"

"I want her monitored by those who can help her way better than you can. Way better than I can. This is for everyone's safety."

"No. She's not—" Terri had a difficult time trying to get the words out. "Amanda's… she's not…"

"Ms. Connors, please. Reconsider this. You're treading into very dangerous waters here."

"She's not a fucking psychotic!" bellowed Terri, taking her by surprise.

"I never said that," said Dr. Sperling, a hand raised in an attempt to calm down the woman sitting across from him. "Our minds are exactly like the body. Just as we can fall ill with a flu or a virus, so can the brain. It can get sick, too. Depression. Anxiety. Obsessive Compulsive Disorder. These are all illnesses of the brain. And they can be treated."

Terri stood up from her chair and stared the doctor down, her lips so tight they were going white. "Get my daughter. Now."

Dr. Sperling didn't move from his chair. Instead, he sat there, looking up at the pissed-off woman. He sighed and reached for the phone. Terri watched him as he picked up the receiver and pressed a button. He talked to someone on the other end, and within minutes, Amanda was escorted into the room, looking rather tired.

"This is a very unwise decision you've just made, Ms. Connors. I hope you reconsider," said the doctor. "And I have it in my power to call CPS and have this child removed from your home."

"I want Violet Red, NOW!" shrieked Amanda, very suddenly.

The doctor stared at Amanda. "Amanda, you get to go home. You can be with your little toys—"

"You fucking fat pig!" screamed Amanda.

He looked back up at Terri, nearly pleading with his eyes. "You can't let her go home like this!"

"Watch me," Terri said, her teeth practically showing. "Why don't you go ahead and call CPS?"

Amanda broke free of the nurse's grasp and ran to the desk. Terri tried to hold her daughter away – she was reaching for a pen. The doctor stood up from where he was sitting, but Amanda pushed her mother away, causing Terri to fall down. She felt so weak. Felt so out of touch. But the pressure applied to her was barely childish. It wasn't even like an adult doing so. It felt like being slammed by a vehicle!

The nurse grabbed Amanda before she could do anything. "You're not taking your daughter home, ma'am."

Terri finally regained her footing and stood up. She wanted to scream out a no, but she couldn't find her voice. She looked at her daughter, squirming in the nurse's tight grip and knew that sometimes loving someone to death meant doing the right thing for them.

TERRI SOBBED AND broke down as soon as she walked back into her house. Delana wasn't there yet. She was all alone with her thoughts, with memories of her daughter swimming laps in her mind.

She remembered the day Amanda was born. She was about eight pounds when she first entered the world. She remembered the look on Jeff's face when he saw his daughter come into the world. He was crying. He looked into the eyes of this newborn and broke down.

"We made this. Together," he whispered in her ear.

"I love you," was all Terri could say, in between tears of joy and pain.

He knelt down and kissed her gently on the cheek. "I know you're talking to this baby girl. I love her just as much as you do. And I love you."

Terri remembered Amanda's first steps. How it took her a while to finally let go and let Amanda walk on her own. She smiled through painful tears as she remembered when Amanda finally conquered the shoelaces. It didn't seem so long ago.

It felt like all those moments happened only months ago.

What could be the source of all this pain? What was the source of this force of hatred and rage?

As soon as Terri regained her composure, she went to the library. Maybe they had something that could help her understand everything. She crossed her fingers as she walked into that large library, walking over to the woman sitting at the front desk who was helping a little girl with her new library card. She gasped as she drew nearer to the desk.

"Amanda?" she found herself asking as she got closer.

"Huh?" The little girl turned around, facing Terri. An adult standing nearby walked over to the child.

Terri took a step back. It clearly wasn't her daughter, but she could've sworn she saw Amanda. "I'm so sorry," she said to the man who placed a hand on his daughter's shoulder. "She looks so much like my daughter. She's very sick and I'm trying to help her."

The man's facial expression changed. "I'm sorry to hear that, ma'am."

It was so inappropriate to do in that moment, but she couldn't help herself. She began sobbing again, for what seemed like the tenth time that day. She told the stranger everything that had happened.

The man placed a hand on Terri's shoulder. "My wife is chronically ill. I know what it's like to have someone so close to you suffering in that way."

"It's not fair," she said, wiping her eyes. "I'm really sorry to put all this on your shoulders. It's been so tough."

The man opened up his arms and gave her a very sincere, warm hug. "If you need to talk, please come by my office." He pulled out his wallet, took out a business card, and handed it to Terri.

She looked at the card. He was a preacher. "Pastor Louis Nygaard," she said out loud. She looked up at him. "Thank you, Pastor."

"Please, call me Louis," he replied.

It looked like he was silently crying with her, which made her feel ten times better than she had all day.

"Louis," she said, smiling. "Thank you."

"Please call soon. I might not have all the answers, but I certainly can provide the best medicine that I can offer, and that's a receptive ear."

Terri stopped for a moment and remembered what Dr. Sperling said earlier. She asked him if he had ever seen the movie, *The Exorcist*. To her surprise, he said that he had.

"Great cinematography," he replied. "And almost accurate."

"What do you mean?" asked Terri.

"Call me later and schedule an appointment, and I'll tell you everything I know."

TERRI DIDN'T MENTION a word about the visit to the library to Delana. She hadn't spoken much to Jeff, either. But she did let him know that Amanda was being taken care of at the children's hospital. At first, he was just as upset as Terri was, but in the end he also realized that her being treated was probably the best thing for their daughter.

She did, however, schedule an appointment with Pastor Nygaard. Delana overheard it, but Terri didn't notice the eavesdropper until after she had placed the phone down on the receiver.

"Why are you scheduling an appointment with a man who believes we're living in sin?" she asked, her lips pursed, hands against her hips.

Terri left the room without speaking. She walked into the kitchen and opened the fridge, looking for something to drink. She pulled out a beer and opened the can.

"Why were you on the phone with a church?" pursued Delana.

Terri sighed and sat down at the kitchen table. "I know Amanda's being taken care of by the children's hospital. But something in my heart believes that it's not a brain thing."

"Of course it's a brain thing, Terri," Delana snapped, now helping herself to a beer. "The idea that a church can help with something like this is antiquated. It's fucking ridiculous."

"I know that," Terri snapped back. "I'm just looking for as many answers as I possibly can. Jesus, Delana!"

"And what exactly are you expecting to hear from this preacher?"

"I don't know. I really don't. If you don't want me to go to his church, then come with me. I just want to talk to him for a few minutes. See what he has to say."

"I'm not coming with you."

"Well, I made an appointment for today in about an hour. So I'll be gone for a bit. While I'm out, I'll pick something up for supper. What do you want?"

"I don't want you to go."

"Chinese or pizza?"

Delana took a drink of her beer. "You're really going to

do this."

"Well, we'll both be hungry by the time I'm out of the church."

Delana slammed her hand down on the table. "Stop this! Stop making a mockery out of this!"

Terri got up from the table and stared down Delana. "If it makes you feel any better than you do now, I had complete intentions on running out of there if he said one terrible thing about gay people. After I slap him across the face."

Delana smiled weakly. "I'm sorry. It's just been really rough here since…"

Terri closed her eyes. Delana was right. It had been very difficult since admitting her daughter to the children's hospital. She couldn't deny that. Their sex life was practically thrown into the dumpster. And they had been eating separately from one another.

Then she got an idea. "How about this? After I'm through at the church, I'll pick you up and we go out to that Mexican restaurant you love so much."

"You hate Mexican."

"I don't hate Mexican. I just don't like spicy food."

Delana laughed for the first time in days. Smiling, she got up from the table and embraced Terri. "You've got forty-five minutes before you have to leave."

Terri got the hint. She slowly kissed Delana on the lips, her tongue slipping inside Delana's mouth. Delana's hands were draped across Terri's outfit, pulling it back to reveal her bare shoulders. Moaning, Terri pushed her against the table and continued making love to her.

Then the phone rang.

"Shit," Terri whispered in Delana's ear. "I'm not answering that."

"Please, don't," Delana begged.

But the phone continued to ring.

"Goddamn it," Terri said as she straightened herself up and went to the phone. Irritably, she answered the phone with a curt "What?"

Jeff was on the other line. "They want Amanda to come home."

"You've got to be joking," Terri said, taking a seat on the couch next to the end table. "I've been talking with the doctors there. No sign of improvement."

"I know," Jeff replied. "You're not the only one talking to them. Are you busy right now?"

Terri came really close to blurting out what she was doing when he called but thought better of it. Instead, she told him that she had a really important appointment.

"Can you cancel it?" asked Jeff.

"I guess so," she replied back, hesitantly.

"I'll be over in about fifteen minutes."

IT SEEMED LIKE less than fifteen minutes. Jeff was there, not bothering to knock on the door. Delana was the one to answer – Terri was in the bathroom cleaning herself up. They had resumed their lovemaking and finally felt as though things were getting back to normal for their relationship.

Terri walked out of the bathroom and offered Jeff something to drink. He gladly accepted a beer.

"I don't know about this," Terri said uncomfortably, holding Delana's hand. "She almost assaulted that carpet cleaner. She's not stable enough to come home."

"We're three grown adults," Jeff said, taking a swig of his drink. "I don't think we're going to die at the hands of a little child. That's just crazy."

Immediately, Terri thought about Amanda's murdered teacher. She cringed at the memory of hearing about Miss Hammett's untimely death.

"He has a point," Delana replied. "But I would feel a lot more comfortable knowing that Amanda is safe, surrounded by people who know what they're doing. I know nothing about child mental disorders. Terri doesn't either."

Terri shook her head in agreement. "This whole damn thing is ludicrous. Why exactly do they want to discharge her?"

Jeff sighed. "They think that the medications are finally working. Amanda's not throwing shit around the rooms. She's not threatening to kill people, and she isn't stabbing them with pencils."

"So now our little girl has to be medicated," Terri said out loud, rubbing her forehead. "Probably for the rest of her life."

The phone rang. Delana answered it, then handed the phone to Terri.

"I'll take this in the bedroom," Terri said as she got up.

It was Pastor Nygaard. "You're still coming, right?"

"Oh shit, I'm sorry," she said. "My ex-husband is here. We just found out our daughter's being discharged."

"She is?" replied Louis, his voice draped in intrigue.

"Um, yeah. She might have to live with her father for the time being. I'm just not…"

"Comfortable with the situation at the moment," he said, finishing her thought.

"That's part of it. Um, I'm really sorry I missed our appointment. Can we reschedule?"

"Would it be better if I came over there instead?" he asked.

Terri hesitated. "Honestly, I don't know if that's such a great idea. My partner isn't very thrilled that I'm even talking with you, and Jeff? I honestly don't know if he'd be willing to talk to you at this point."

"I can understand that. It would help me immensely, though, to get all the information I can."

"Can I call you back? I need to ask them if it's all right if you stopped by."

She didn't wait for him to respond. She disconnected the line and walked back into the living room. "So, that was a preacher at a local church here. Louis Nygaard. He wants to come over and talk to all of us."

"He's okay with coming over to a lesbian's home?" Delana asked, dumbfounded.

"That poor guy," Jeff muttured.

"So is this a yes or a no? I told him I'd call back after asking."

"You must be losing your senses. He's not coming here," Delana said irritably.

"That's all I needed to hear," Terri said as she dialed his number. He was on another call, so she relayed the answer to the church secretary.

"You didn't want him over here, did you?" Jeff asked, half smiling.

"I'm just as hesitant to talk with him for the same reason Delana doesn't want me at the church," Terri admitted.

"I knew it!" exclaimed Delana. "So why are you still wanting to talk to the man?"

"This is going to sound ridiculous, but the doctors compared her symptoms to Reagan MacNeil from—"

Jeff cut her off. "*The Exorcist*? You're joking, right?"

"She was cursing and attacking the nurses and even the doctor. I saw her go after the doctor, Jeff. I didn't want her to go into the hospital. I didn't. But when you see it actually happen? You realize that you're in a losing game with something," Terri snapped. "I just don't know what I'm losing to."

"And you think that talking to a priest would do what, exactly?" asked Delana, now understanding why Terri scheduled that appointment. This was the first time she actually talked about that ill-fated doctor's appointment.

"Honestly, I really don't know. I just wanted his opinion. That's really it."

"I can't believe I'm about to do this," Delana said, "but if you need to talk to him about this, you've got my blessing."

"So he can come here?"

"No," Delana replied. "But you can meet him wherever. But promise me that you will run out of there the moment anything homophobic happens. Please."

"You have my word. I promise."

TERRI WASN'T SURE what to expect when she finally pulled into the parking lot of the church. When she was driving, she imagined a tall building, with pillars and angels in the engravings. No. This was nothing like she expected, at all. For a moment, when she entered into the parking lot, she thought she was at the wrong place. Before she left her car, she looked at the building and remembered that it used to be a funeral home. She silently giggled to herself, laughing at the irony.

She left the car, the sound of her shoes making that clack-clack noise as she crossed into the entryway. Pulling on the handle, she realized the door was locked.

She swore. She let him know she was on her way, and he said it was fine. She stopped pulling – clearly that wasn't getting her anywhere – and stopped to look around.

Out of the corner of her eyes, she saw a familiar person come into her line of sight. She could see him say something but wasn't sure what he was saying.

Louis Nygaard let her in, apologizing profusely for the doors being locked. "I told her to make sure the doors didn't lock right before she left. I'm so sorry for that!"

Terri forced herself to smile. "It's okay. We all have those moments, don't we?"

Louis laughed. "Yeah, I guess we do," he replied as he led her down the hall and into what looked like a large room set for office space. It was minimalistic, but there were just a few religious items scattered around. She wondered who made the unfortunate decision to put two crosses right next to a picture of White Jesus. She turned away, allowing Louis to lead her to his office.

He opened the door, extending his arm to a nice large, blue sofa. He opened the fridge and pulled out a can of soda. "Would you like one?"

She declined. Instead of placing it back in the fridge, he cracked it open, took a sip, then placed it on his desk. Terri nearly flinched – he didn't even bother with a coaster! She looked up at him. "All right. Tell me what you know."

Louis took another drink before he reached over to pick up a book he had on his desk. "I'm turning that command over to you, Terri. Tell me what you know."

Terri hesitated before she got into even more details of what was ailing her young daughter. At times, she glanced nervously at the clock, particularly when she told him about her relationship with Delana and how Amanda was getting so close to her.

"That's very unfortunate. Forgive me for how this sounds, but do you think maybe she's just adjusting to the situation? I mean, she is used to having a male in the house along with you."

Terri opened her mouth to dispute this ridiculous claim, but he raised his hand before she could reply. "I don't intend to sound as though being in a house with two women is the cause of her distress. All I am saying is that this was a huge shift for her. She was used to her father being with her, 24/7. I believe that strong relationships come from having a strong parental chemistry between a child and their parents. Now that she is seeing less of him than she's been used to, that has made a slight, or maybe even a bigger, impression upon Amanda."

Terri was rather flabbergasted by such a remark by a pastor. "Okay, just saying this, but I did not expect that kind of response from you."

"And what exactly were you expecting?"

Terri laughed. "I expected you to say something along the lines of, 'woman and woman should not be together.' That we are an abomination in the eyes of the Lord Jesus Christ.

That our 'sin' was the cause of Amanda's illness."

Louis leaned in, almost dramatically. "Between you and me," he said almost whisper-like, "considering that God took a rib out of Adam to make him feel less alone, it really *was* Adam and Steve, not Adam and Eve. But you didn't hear that from me." He winked at her.

Terri grinned. She liked him, almost venerated the man! "Hear what?" she playfully asked.

Louis retained his smile, albeit briefly. "Conflict. There's no escaping it. Now, this is just my theory, and I have nothing to back it up, since I've never met your daughter. But considering what your daughter probably knew when the roles changed and when your girlfriend entered the picture, she was more than likely very shocked. Not traumatized, just shocked. It's very possible she never fully processed the change in the home. Now she has three adults in her life – you, your ex-husband, and your girlfriend. Yes, she has more adults to confide in, and she has a second home, but inside her little mind, there is a plea for there to be just one house, with those adults living in harmony. From what you have told me, I think that her reaction may have something to do with the environment.

"You also told me in confidence about Ida. I'm so sorry she passed, but since your daughter never got to give a final good-bye to this woman who verbally harmed her, she's also trying to process the sudden loss of an abuser. A child's mind can only process so many things at once before it finally starts to become ill. It's like adding an extra wheel to grind, but the mechanism to help the wheel along is too small for that new wheel.

"All these things, working in tandem inside of your daughter's mind, may be the root cause of all the horror you've seen lately. Maybe she tried to attack the carpet cleaner because it was symbolic of him bringing out all her hurt and pain out into the open? I will say there's that possibility.

"But then you tell me that the doctors have already done what they could to figure out just what exactly is ailing your daughter, Terri. I think there's something else. Something much more nefarious working. Any ethical man of God would tell you that you must seek your answers steeped in the world around you – science, in other words. Eliminate all your natural conclusions before you reach your supernatural conclusions, if you will. I don't know exactly what may have been that—"

He suddenly stopped talking. Terri noticed it, as well. Right above the desk was a beautiful ceiling fan, and it started spinning on its own. The switch to turn the fan on was across the room. Even though Terri was immersed in Louis's theories, she knew he was getting hot. He was getting to the actual root of the problem.

Terri swallowed nervously. "Please tell me that's remote controlled, and you're messing with me."

But there was no remote in sight.

"As I was saying," he continued, pretending not to notice the oddity, "demons are never uninvited. They're always invited. And when this happens, it's never of our own volition."

"That makes no sense," Terri replied, still looking at the fan, which was still running.

"The Devil is also known as the Great Deceiver," Louis said, stealing a glance at the fan, which was now running faster than it was a moment ago. "He will find ways. I find the Ouija board to be a dangerous, yet fascinating, method. It's marketed as just a silly game for children to play at slumber parties, but if someone has certain intentions, that little piece of plastic can invite something in. Has your daughter ever done anything with a Ouija board?"

"I'll admit, I did have one at one point, but she knew nothing of it."

"I think otherwise," Louis said, still staring at the fan, which had now reduced its speed. "Children are natural explorers. It's how they learn. I would bet money that your daughter – and don't tell my boss I'm betting $50 on this – that your daughter knew of that board and played with it. I can't say why, but I do know that the why is rooted in curiosity, if anything. You said that at one point you had it. Where is it now?"

Terri swallowed nervously, again. "I am selling it at my antique store."

He didn't even flinch when she said those words. "Has anyone bought it yet?"

"No," she said after thinking for a second. "Nobody has."

"I need you to bring it in. Immediately."

"I honestly don't think the board has anything to do with all this. I really don't."

Louis regarded the woman sitting on the couch for a moment as he considered anything else which may have brought the theorized demon into her home. He stole glances of her outfit. It was simple, like the four walls around him. She wore a somewhat loose shirt, a light blue color. No design, but simple. He couldn't help but wonder if this was normal clothing for Terri. He considered her to wear something more colorful and more suitable to her personality, but the more he thought about what her true personality was, the louder it became.

He could see in his mind Terri smiling and laughing along with her daughter and her life partner. He couldn't help but smile along as he saw three happy young women enjoying their lives at home. In his mind, Terri wasn't wearing a plain, light blue shirt. No, she was wearing something more elaborate, but also modest. The illness Amanda had been inflicted with was also slowly affecting Terri, sinking her down into her vulnerabilities, to make her feel worthless and rundown.

It was confirmation enough as he realized this wasn't Terri he was talking to. The woman sitting on his sofa was at her wits end, her personality and natural color draining. The demon already infested Amanda, but how? The demon already was oppressing other members – he thought of what she said about the strange dreams. Demons were artists when it came to frightening nightmares. That was no surprise to him. This thing had also lashed out at Delana, or at least attempted to make its mark upon her. Having to step in to help her significant other was apparently jarring enough for her, but somehow she still kept her wits together. There was a strength in Delana, one he admired her for.

But then he remembered something Terri had said.

"All this started after I gifted her that stuffed dog I found at my store," he remembered.

It couldn't have been the board.

At the same time, an energy strong enough to use a stuffed animal as a conduit could also pass on some of its zeal into other objects, if it had the energy to do so.

Terri's voice interrupted his thoughts. "Louis?"

Louis adjusted his sight and looked back into her eyes. "You mentioned a toy your daughter named Violet Red. I don't think you told me just exactly where that toy is."

"She brought it to school with her, the day her teacher was killed. I heard the police took the toy."

"From what I heard, this toy was blood-stained, is that correct?"

"Yes. They think the killer dropped the toy when he fled the property."

"I think that the toy is a conduit," Louis said, without thinking as he finally opened the book he grabbed from the surface of his desk. Terri listened carefully as Louis explained that a conduit is an object used as a way for demonic spirits to stay on the earthly plain. Normal items such as dolls and even necklaces, can be used as a way for these entities to come and go. What was particularly striking to Terri was when Louis said that for an item to become a conduit for something vile, some kind of sacrifice was used to "open the gates of Hell." Terri shuddered to think about what could have been done to allow something so innocent and cute to be a pipeline to the demonic.

According to the book he was reading from, when vulnerable people, like children, grow too attached to those objects, it has the potential to cross over and create havoc, to the point of something even worse than she ever imagined.

"First comes obsession," Louis said quietly.

"I don't want to know what comes after that," Terri confessed.

Louis could only stare back at her, his sympathy comforting her like a blanket on a cold night. "Let's just hope it's not possession," he finally said. "Thank, and praise God, that the toy is away from her."

-14-

For at least three days when Amanda came home from the children's hospital, things were quiet, yet foreboding. Amanda still was not her normal self, but Terri and Delana were grateful for the silence, despite the odd feeling that anything could happen at any moment. Amanda had been oddly subdued – nothing was grabbing her attention and she hardly reacted to anything, like the sound of a kitchen cabinet closing loudly or Delana's usual loud sneezing. Her peculiar way of sternutation always sparked a giggle from Amanda.

Late one night, while they were seated on the couch and watching television, Amanda slowly turned her head to Terri. "This show is boring," she said to her tonelessly.

Terri couldn't help but agree. "Let's find something else."

"There's nothing else on," remarked Delana, picking up the remote from the arm rest. "But I can see if there's something else that might catch your attention."

"Okay," Amanda replied serenely.

For a few minutes, nothing really seemed to grab anybody's attention. As the television showed someone crying out in pain, Amanda gasped.

"Can we watch this?" asked Amanda excitedly.

"It looks too scary," replied Delana as she reached for a handful of popcorn.

But she begged to watch the scary movie. They didn't want to have to deal with another temper tantrum, so they ended up watching the movie. Terri felt uncomfortable, sitting on the couch and watching the screen, also noticing just how unfazed Amanda was. She seemed to be watching with gross intensity, almost to the point where Amanda was scaring her way more than the weird creature-looking thing tearing into a teenager.

She closed her eyes, trying to focus on something else, but the task proved to be rather daunting to her. The voices on the screen and the distorted voice of the creature were too distracting to attempt to do anything in that moment.

The sensation of a small hand on her arm nearly made her jump. "Mom?" her daughter asked timidly. There was something in that voice that reminded her of her child before this strange ailment.

Terri turned her head to face her daughter.

"Mom? I'm scared."

"We can watch something else. Or do you want to go to bed?" asked Terri. "Maybe it's time for bed."

"I'm not scared of the show," Amanda said, still rather quietly. "I'm scared because I *like this show*."

Terri looked at her daughter. "Come on, honey. Let's go to bed."

Amanda yawned and stood up. Terri followed her to her room. Her daughter climbed into bed, pulling the comforter over her tiny body. "I'm sorry."

Terri looked at her daughter the way a mother should. Instead of the fear and terror made up on her face, it was love and sympathy. "What are you sorry for?"

"I'm sorry for—"

The room got cold. Terri shivered.

Then the screaming began.

She looked down at her daughter. She was shaking from the cold.

No, she wasn't shaking from the cold.

She was convulsing!

Terri yelled for Delana as she tried to calm Amanda down. She was sobbing uncontrollably, her limbs flailing, threatening to hit her mother. Her head twitched from left to right, then right to left, as though an unseen force was trying to snap it right off her little neck. It was almost petrifying to watch, but Terri knew she had to do something. She just didn't know what to do, other than freeze and watch.

Delana rushed into the room and stopped before heading to the bed. "Oh my God!"

Then everything went quiet. Delana slowly approached the foot of the bed, afraid to do anything that could initiate another attack.

Instead, there was a low laugh coming out of Amanda's lips. Both of the adults were expecting something to speak, but it was just a cynical laugh.

"We need to get her to a hospital," murmured Delana.

Terri agreed. This was insane. This was absolutely mortifying, watching her daughter go through what looked like a seizure. Just as she was about to reach to grab her daughter, Amanda jerked away.

But it didn't seem like Amanda was doing that willingly. The way she pulled away wasn't normal. It was like something was tugging on her little body, keeping her away from two adults who loved and doted on this little, innocent child.

No matter what, Terri couldn't reach out and grab her daughter. Even when Delana stood on the other side, she tried to grab her, but it was as though there was some kind of wall around her, something attempting to keep Amanda away from her parents.

"The girl is mine," something hissed out of Amanda's mouth.

But they didn't give up, no matter the curses being thrown their way. They finally were able to grab ahold of her, drag her out of the room and into the car.

IT WAS UNFORTUNATE for him, that by the time he arrived at Terri's home, they were already on their way out. He could sense something was wrong as he approached the driver's side and knocked gently on the glass. Looking inside, Ian saw a woman wearing fear and anxiety on her face.

"This isn't a good time," Terri said hurriedly. "My daughter is very ill. I have to go."

He could hear something yelling from the back seat. Looking through, he couldn't help but notice a pale-faced child glaring at him. Delana snapped her head back to see what Ian was looking at.

"What's wrong?" he asked the child.

But Amanda could only glare at him. She was about to say something, but something made her close her lips and just glare at him.

"Seriously, Detective. We have to go. If you need anything, just stay here. We'll be back," Terri persisted in trying to leave.

"Is it okay if I look around the house? I have a warrant."

Delana practically jolted out of the car and unlocked the house. Ian was rather shocked she did this. "Fine. But we need to leave. Do whatever the hell you want!" she yelled.

Before Ian could protest and say one of them needed to be present, the car left, leaving him behind. Having never been in a situation like this, he called and asked if he should just wait, or if he could go in, since he had their permission.

"Tread carefully," was all he was told.

He entered the home, turning on the lights. He knew he was alone, since everybody had left, but he could feel something else with him. Automatically, he posed his gun.

"This is the Grand Rapids Police Department. Whoever is here, show yourself."

But he felt as though he was talking to nobody but himself. Not wanting to take any chances, he kept his gun aimed, in the case of an intruder. He walked around the home slowly, making sure to capture all places where someone could be hiding.

As he approached the hallway, he could hear soft whispering coming from one of the rooms. Once again, he announced himself, telling anybody who may be in any of the rooms who he was. He felt his body growing colder as he approached the end of the hallway.

Slowly, he opened the door to one of the rooms. He was surprised at just how cold the room was. It was like he walked right into a freezer. Shivering, he kept his gun pointed. As he neared the bed, he saw something silvery shining from the corner of the pillow. Carefully, he lifted the little pillow and was horrified to see the same bloody scissors used to kill the teacher. By now, it had dried and became a part of the weapon.

How was this possible? he asked himself.

The weapon was taken into police custody, but he knew that pair of scissors. He knew it by heart. But it certainly was a mystery how it was here.

Sighing, he put on his gloves, placed the scissors in the bag, and left the room. He wondered how this could've been possible. But he knew he finally found their killer.

But why would her mother slip it under her daughter's pillow? He would have to ask her, once he took her in for questioning.

AMANDA HAD ONCE again been admitted to the hospital. Terri and Delana took seats in the room Amanda occupied, waiting for someone to tell them what was wrong with her. The tests had taken almost an hour and a half of their time, and they were anxious to hear what the doctors had to say. Finally, Dr. Jones came in, looking tired and exhausted. He was a slightly balding man close to his mid-fifties and had a problem with keeping his horn-rimmed glasses where they should be.

"For now, let's just assume she's epileptic," the doctor said as he adjusted the glasses for the hundredth time that day, but Terri was so numb she wasn't exactly completely listening to his words. "We're keeping her for at least three days while we find out what's exactly wrong. No sign of concussion, but I'm very worried about her safety."

"Three days," murmured Delana. "Three days of waiting. We're used to waiting, doctor." Her voice suddenly grew even more agitated and irate. "But we're sick and tired of not getting adequate answers for what's wrong with our daughter! We're getting fucking tired of not knowing what is going on! We're getting sick of not knowing what we can do to… to…"

She drew in a deep breath and let it go in seconds. "We just want answers. I'm sorry for freaking out."

The doctor looked at her gravely. "She's not your daughter by blood."

Delana saw red and jumped out of her chair, not noticing an officer just walked into the room. Ian held her back from killing the guy, simply for doing his job.

"Woah there!" Ian yelled at her. "Don't make me arrest you!"

Delana glared at him. A male nurse came pounding into the hospital room and told them if they couldn't keep quiet, everyone would have to leave. Terri shot a tired, apologetic look at the nurse, and the nurse looked over to Dr. Jones. He returned the look back to Terri, as though understanding why the screaming match had even begun. Then he left the room.

Ian looked at the little body on the hospital bed. Clearing his throat, he turned his head to the doctor. "What's the prognosis?" he asked him calmly.

"Possibly epilepsy," he replied, nervously looking over at Delana, who was still shaking in fury.

"She won't harm you," Ian reassured the older gentleman. He watched as the doctor pushed his glasses up. He didn't need to do that, considering that the glasses didn't need to be readjusted. "They're just very worried about their daughter."

"That woman is not her mother by blood."

Now it was Ian's turn to glare at the man. "She helps take care of Amanda, doesn't she? She helps feed the girl. She ensures that this girl is safe and sound in a home, doesn't she?"

The doctor didn't return Ian's glance.

"Ian, please," Terri rasped. "It's okay."

"No, it's not," Ian snapped. "This doctor doesn't know shit."

"Excuse me?" the doctor replied, sounding offended. "I have had years of—"

"I don't give two shits where you got your medical degrees and that you were valedictorian or whatever shit education you received," Ian hissed. "You do not treat people like that. How dare you."

The doctor didn't respond but instead, cleared his throat, his lips quivering. "Three days. I'll do whatever I can to make sure she receives the best care."

Then he nearly ran out of that hospital room, not looking back.

DOCTOR JONES' WORDS pierced Delana and sank into her bone marrow as she drove away from the hospital. As she started on the road back home, she sorrowfully glanced over at the passenger side and then quickly looked behind her. It was dark outside, and she felt out in the open. She felt alone and vulnerable, going back home without anyone else in the car with her.

Ian had arrested Terri a few minutes after the doctor had left. At that point, Delana felt defeated. She didn't even react or say anything as the detective led Terri out of the hospital in handcuffs. Following behind, Delana saw the eyes of several onlookers, one of which was the bigoted doctor whispering in hushed voices to another nurse, who looked as though she would rather be elsewhere.

She didn't want to go home, but there wasn't any option for her. She drove past a strip club and thought for a moment about going in, just to get a drink in her. She suddenly stopped the vehicle and turned around, allowing herself to feel something. She needed to feel something, whether it was alcohol permeating inside of her or just an "accidental" touch from a patron.

She walked into the doors of The Basement and looked around. It looked like the club had seen better days. The walls were a judgmental blue, covered in posters of X-rated porn stars who had, or still did, worked here. She slowly walked to a little table tucked away in the corner.

A tall, red-haired woman, wearing a bright green brassiere smiled her way and took her order. Delana didn't realize just how hungry she was and ordered an order of mozzarella sticks and chicken wings, along with a beer. She didn't notice the guy sitting next to her, ogling her as though she was a piece of candy. He picked up his drink and walked over to her.

"A woman in a strip club that's fully clothed? Is this the end of days?" he asked, grinning. Delana could smell the alcohol on his breath.

Delana rolled her eyes. "If you're looking for a show, you're not gonna get it from me."

"Name's Emmett. What's yours, darling?"

"Not-Your-Type," she responded, thanking the waitress who came around with her beer. She took a drink.

"Oh, come on. Join me and my friends at the table. I promise, we don't bite."

"No thanks."

Emmett stared at her. "I said, we don't bite. Get your ass off that chair and join my friends."

"I said, no!" she exclaimed.

"Is this guy bugging you?" another guy asked,

approaching the table rather quickly. "Leave the woman alone, Emmett. She's not interested."

Emmett glared at the guy who cock-blocked him, grabbing him by the shirt. "You stay the fuck outta this."

The waitress who had served her knew something was going on and punched him on the side of his face. "Get out of here! You know the rules!"

"He's three sheets to the wind – he doesn't even know the rules anymore!" someone else shouted. Delana couldn't help but laugh at the retort.

"Screw you, you bitch."

"The name's Jewell!" she cried as what looked like a bouncer grabbed Emmett, throwing him out of the club.

Jewell sighed and looked over at Delana, who was grinning and sipping her beer, as though nothing had happened. "I'm so sorry for that, dear. He's a regular who shouldn't be one."

Delana sat her glass down on the table. "No worries. I suppose, in a place like this, you get that quite a bit."

Jewell laughed. "Every weekend, almost. And always around this time of the night." She regarded the customer with a strange look, then asked, "We usually don't get women customers here. It's almost always white men in their late thirties and beyond. What brings you here?"

Delana wasn't sure how to respond at first. She took another drink and shook her head. "Oh, I don't know. It's just been one of those days. No, scratch that. It's been a very stressful couple weeks."

"So you decided to come here, with a bunch of women basically shaking their tits at horny old men," mused Jewell, still confused.

"It's kinda, umm, almost nostalgic for me," Delana replied.

"Nostalgic?"

"Yeah. Nostalgic. It's basically your typical 'college girl is poor and needs money' story. I used to dance and do some waiting for this place. It's been years since I've been back."

"No way," Jewell said, her jaw dropping. "You used to dance for us?"

Delana snorted. "Not the best decision of my life, but no judgment from me. I respect those that work here. It was here that I realized that I wasn't really into the clientele, if you know what I mean."

Jewell scratched her arm. "As in, older men?"

"As in, men in general."

It suddenly dawned on Jewell what Delana was referring to. She lowered herself down to the customer and whispered, "Neither am I."

Delana felt comfortable around Jewell. She couldn't help but think about how beautiful she was. It wasn't just her breasts that caught her attention, but her whole demeaner. Jewell didn't seem to give a shit about anything and could stand up for herself.

And she also probably wasn't dealing with a sick daughter or a too-exhausted girlfriend, either.

"I used to love the attention," Delana continued, "and the tips were perfect. But then there was this guy who obsessed over me. Stalked me and everything. If it hadn't have been for my RA and my best friend, I don't know what I would've done. That's when I finally left this place."

"Creeps," Jewell said.

"Creeps."

The women were silent for a while, then someone shouted over to Jewell, screaming about a food order. It turned out to be Delana's. She placed it gently down on the table and took a seat next to her. She offered the waitress a mozzarella stick, and she gladly accepted.

"Shouldn't you be working?" asked Delana, swallowing a bite of chicken. It was just as she remembered – slightly burnt, but the ranch dressing made up for it.

"I already am," Jewell said, looking over at the bar. "Nobody really comes in here for the bar food or even the drinks. That, and there's always at least two others here. I mean, look around you. We're not exactly the most popular place here in town. What was it like when you were here?"

Delana took a drink of her beer before she answered, "Kinda like this? But it was just an inch or two busier than it is here."

Jewell laughed. "I like the way you have with words."

Delana looked over at Jewell. She knew this woman was flirting with her, and as wrong as it felt, it also felt so right. She longed for this kind of attention. God knows how long Terri was going to be in custody.

Jewell reached a hand over to her and placed it on her arm. "But there's something else. You don't seem happy. You look like you are in the middle of a battle."

Delana hesitated for a while. Jewell's touch lingered on her arm. She wasn't being overtly sensual with her. It was just a hand on her arm. But she may as well have started rubbing her arm, touching the fabric of her shirt as though it wasn't covering her skin. She finally told her about what was going on at home, and mistakenly told her about the issues she'd been having with Terri. Jewell hung on to every word.

"Doctors can be such twats, sometimes," Jewell said as Delana finished sharing about what happened at the hospital. "You're just as much a mother to that sweet girl as Terri is."

"Thank you!" exclaimed Delana. She didn't realize just how loud her voice was, but it was nice to have someone so sensible listening to her.

"Tell you what," Jewell said, standing up. "The drink's on me, but you need to pay for your food."

Delana laughed. "Sounds fair to me." She reached into her pocket and pulled out her wallet, taking out a $20 bill. She handed it to Jewell. She left to make the change. When Jewell came back, she handed her $15.00, and a slip of paper with her home phone number on it.

"Umm, I should have received $10 back," Delana said, pocketing the phone number. She shouldn't have accepted that slip of paper, but she would have to make sure to set boundaries, despite the feeling that she didn't want them. She couldn't help but think about Jewell in that way. She wanted to experience more of Jewell's warm touch, longed to feel Jewell slipping her tongue inside of her. She almost squirmed in pleasure thinking about Jewell and the power she potentially carried in her flesh.

"I ate most of those sticks, girl. You just paid for the chicken wings." Jewell winked at her, then placed her hand on Delana's shoulder. "I hope you get everything worked out. And I hope you stop in again. Maybe you could…"

Delana knew what Jewell was asking. "I don't strip anymore. But thanks."

"Pity," Jewell replied back, smirking. "You've got one beautiful body."

DOCTOR JONES SAT at his desk, taking his glasses off. He thought about Amanda, wondering about what was possibly ailing her. He was convinced she was epileptic and wondered if there was something else going on in that sinful home. He prayed quickly for Amanda, for healing. He prayed that Delana would repent of her homosexuality. At the same time, he couldn't help but think just how amazingly sexy she was, when she got in his face.

He coughed into his handkerchief and folded it on his desk, making sure that the corners of the handkerchief were touching as he gently patted it down. He got up from his desk and applied hand sanitizer on his hands. It had been at least an hour after the incident in Amanda's room, and he thought that it would be a good idea for him to check her out himself. He struggled with the male nurse assigned to her, thinking that the young man's nature would actually be more harmful to her than if she had a female nurse.

That's the way it should be, he thought angrily. Men weren't meant to be nurses. They were supposed to be the doctors, the ones in charge. HR was absolutely delusional, thinking about hiring men to do what should be woman's work. Then again, he couldn't help but agree with everyone else that Andrew did a great job and went above and beyond his basic requirements. He wanted to sit down with the guy and find out if he would be interested in pursuing something more attuned to his gender.

He walked out of his office and walked into Amanda's room. She was sleeping in the little bed, maybe dreaming about being back home with her real mother and playing with her Barbies and stuffed animals.

He was confused when he walked over to Amanda's bedside and saw a stuffed dog. He knew that she didn't come with any toys. And he certainly didn't see any stuffed dogs with Terri or Delana. He reached a hand over to the puppy's paws, touching the red ribbon.

He leaped back in pain. Something had pricked him. He grabbed the toy out from under Amanda's arm, tossing it across the room, and she groaned. She blinked her eyes, acknowledging the doctor standing by her side.

"You're gonna die," a voice said from her mouth, but it wasn't a girlish, child's voice that spoke to him. "You're gonna die."

Dr. Jones knew this wasn't normal. Nothing could explain this. He thought about shouting for a nurse but thought better to do so. He looked back at the girl, who was now humming something in her own voice. He leaned closer, to hear what she was humming. The humming then swelled into something with words:

Two little girls, dressed in red.
One girl alive, the other one dead.
Don't close your eyes, don't rest your head.
She is coming for you, the dead girl in red.

The light in the room went out at the last phrase of this terrifying song. A sharp pain came over his chest. He clutched at his heart, staring wide eyed at the little girl, who was now sitting on the side of the bed, grinning at him. He watched in terror as her face changed, as her outfit changed. She was no longer wearing the hospital garments, but a bright, blood-red shirt. Her face contorted, changing colors before his eyes. She had first come into the room pale faced and stricken, but her color had returned, but not in the way it should have.

He groaned as he reached for the side of the bed, but the girl sitting on the hospital bed so contentedly grabbed something he couldn't see, and stabbed him, pushing the object closer to him. He cried out in pain. He hoped someone would hear him, but the door had closed. Aside from the pain he was feeling in his heart, and the pain of being stabbed at, he felt cold. He looked up at the girl, but now the girl was no longer present.

Something else was sitting on the bed, but it wasn't human.

It threw him across the room and lunged at him, its long razer-like fingers tearing into him. He screamed for help, but nobody came.

When the night nurse came around to do her rounds, she saw Dr. Jones lying at the side of Amanda's bed. But there were no claw marks on his body. The nurse shouted, "The witch is dead!" then walked out of the room to get help. She was too surprised to notice that the person who really should have been in that room was no longer there.

-15-

In all the time Ian McBride had worked for the police department, he had never seen the amount of murder that had happened recently. It was jarring. It was emotionally draining. He laid in bed for at least ten minutes before beginning his day, thinking about Terri. Thinking about Amanda. Thinking about his deceased partner.

He stole a glance at the side of his bed, thankful for the first time in his life he wasn't married or dating anyone. He didn't want them to have to go through the stress and anxiety of being involved with a police officer. They'd be up half the night, pacing back and forth. Wondering if Ian would come back home. Fearing for their lives when they knew that maybe a domestic situation could go awry.

There was no way he could put a woman through that. No way. He was lucky in certain ways, he thought to himself as he ran the water in the shower. Divorced with no children, Mickey (when he was alive) no longer had to worry about the things Ian was fretting over today. He remembered a conversation he had with Mickey a while ago. He said something along the lines of a divorced police officer being a godsend to all ex-wives. Bobbi, his ex-wife, constantly obsessed over Mickey's safety, despite the repetitious reassurances that everything would be fine. He was half-right, supposed Ian, as he began shaving his now prominent sideburns. Chuckling to himself about all the goofy times he had with his partner, he wasn't paying attention to the razor, which had pricked him.

Ian swore. He yanked off a square of toilet paper and began to dab at it, while his other hand reached into the cabinet. He pulled out the box of Band-aids and applied one to his face.

The phone rang. He walked out of the bathroom, obsessively patting the bandage on his face. He picked up the phone and greeted his unexpected caller.

"You're going to want to come down as soon as possible," said the voice on the other line.

Ian's attention suddenly perked. "What's going on?"

"I gotta get back to this, but here's the short story version – the blood on this knife is nothing like I've seen," the technician said.

"Ten minutes," Ian said before placing the phone down on the cradle.

"AS YOU CAN see here," Frank said in his teacher-voice, "the blood on this knife doesn't even come close to matching Ginger Hammett's. It doesn't even match up with any of the other victims of this killer."

"But it has to be someone's blood. Someone killed by this guy," Ian said, staring hard at the murder weapon.

"That's the thing, though. This blood isn't human," Frank said, furrowing his brow. "I mean, it looks human at first glance, but take a look at this sample under the microscope."

Ian obliged the technician and took a glance in the microscope. He pretended as though he knew about blood and murmured something, to make it sound as though he knew what he was looking at.

"Right," replied Frank. "There's no white blood cells. No plasma. It's all red blood cells. I've never seen anything like this before."

"That is weird," Ian said while Frank picked something up from the workstation and used it to manipulate the blood sample. Ian watched with fascination as Frank directed him back to the microscope. "Quickly. Take a look at the sample now."

What Ian saw was unusual. The red blood cells, which were scattered, were now furiously scattering all over the slide. They acted provoked, acting erratically and furiously. "I don't know where this blood came from, but it's definite cause for further research," Frank solemnly said to Ian.

"Do what you gotta do," Ian said as his beeper started going off. He walked his way over to the desk phone on Frank's desk and called the number beeping at him.

"There's been another murder," his partner told him over the phone.

"I WANT THIS person jailed!" the sergeant exclaimed. "The number of murders in this town is unacceptable! Tell me, McBride, why you haven't nailed this guy yet!"

It wasn't a question. Caleb Nordquist had every right to be upset and angered by the current situation. It felt as though, since day one, that whoever was committing these atrocities was leading him on a bloody maze with tons of dead ends.

"We thought we had him!" yelled Ian. "We were absolutely certain that Biff was our killer. He knew both Ida and the woman and the daughter who were kidnapped. But then when he was in custody, another murder happened. It couldn't have been him!"

"But then," hissed the sergeant, "then you arrested that antique nut, because you found the murder weapon underneath the pillow of her retarded daughter."

Ian stood up, raging. "She's not retarded!"

"I don't care if she's the goddamn 90s version of Einstein!

Sit the fuck down! Know your place!" Nordquist bellowed. "I don't give two shits what you do. Give that lesbo the death penalty. Then those murders will end."

"But it wasn't her!" Ian yelled. "She's been in custody! The death of the doctor occurred after the fact!"

"I'm not referring to her, you dummy."

"You think Delana did something? Her alibi checks out!"

"They're lesbians," Caleb countered. "Perverts. You know as well as I do that those who commit crime are usually those who have been rightfully marginalized. They don't deserve to walk the same sidewalks as we do. You find her and arrest her."

"I will not," Ian said.

"You do as you're told, d'you hear me?"

Ian got into Caleb's face, which caught the sergeant by surprise. "Both me and my partner went to that strip club. Not only did Jewell verify the fact, but so did two other customers who weren't even drunk. Screw you. I will not arrest Delana simply for being a lesbian."

"Both Delana and Terri earn enough money where they could buy off a ton of people and feed them lies," Caleb sneered. "I'm pretty sure that Delana probably bought them a couple drinks, telling them 'cover for me, please? I need to kill this jackass.' I mean, look at the people who go to strip clubs! You honestly think they're moral? Think they're upstanding citizens?"

"I think we need to be focusing our energy on the missing girl," Ian said, hoping the change of subject would distract him. Luckily for him, it worked.

"Right. Yes. Of course. Although I'm convinced she ran out of that hospital, frightened and terrified. But how did she slip by a ton of hospital staff? I'd talk with that ex-husband, Griff, or whatever his name is."

"Jeff," Ian muttured.

"Go and talk with him," Cliff said, taking a seat at his desk. "And maybe you're right. Obviously, Terri didn't kill the doctor. But Delana? Question her. She clearly has motive."

THEY EMBRACED. HAVING Terri in custody was a jarring moment for Delana. But when she was cleared, when the officers realized the murderer was still at large, that it was not Terri, it was a refreshing moment. Delana felt guilty about her trip to The Basement and told Terri about it. She didn't seem too upset; instead, she understood. In fact, she more than understood. For some reason, Delana's confession turned her on. They slipped into the bedroom.

But the beautiful moment was soon interrupted. Right when they turned off the lights and slipped under the warm comforter, a crashing noise coming from Amanda's bedroom made them jump. They rushed out of the room.

Amanda was in her room, black candles surrounding her. Violet Red was front and center of Amanda, reminding Terri of a picture she had seen in an occult book when she was younger. The candle flames danced around the little girl as she whispered to the toy. Neither of the adults were able to make out what she was saying, but it was enough to warrant ending this disturbing scene.

"Amanda," Terri said in shock as she approached the candles. A strong gust of wind knocked her down. The candles remained untouched, as though they were the ones to call upon the ghastly wind.

"Two little girls, dressed in red. One girl alive, the other one dead. Don't close your eyes, don't rest your head. She is here, the dead girl in red," rasped something coming from the dark corners of the room. For a moment, Delana thought she saw another child in the room, dressed in red.

Terri attempted to stand up, but something was holding her down. Delana tried to help her up, but her grip wasn't strong enough to help her. Something was keeping Terri from intervening. "Call Pastor Nygaard!" cried Terri.

Delana ran out of the room in terror, picking up the phone. Terri had left the pastor's phone number nearby. She grabbed it, her hands shaking. She fumbled over the numbers, accidentally hitting wrong numbers in the process. Finally, she reached him. She told him what was going on, and just as he was about to respond, informing her that he was on his way, the line disconnected.

And so did the electricity.

She was surrounded in darkness, overwhelmed by the horror of the evening. She felt eyes upon her, watching her every move. Listening to every breath she emitted from her lungs.

Nervously, her eyes darted around. She moved slowly, ever so slowly. *What was going on?* she asked herself.

You know what's going on, said something in the room.

"Wh-who w-was that?" she asked aloud.

She is mine.

"She is not yours!"

You dyke. She's been mine since the moment her human flesh touched my toy.

Delana refused to respond, clearing her mind of any thoughts that could potentially give ammo to this mysterious, dark figure.

You are not her mother. You have never been her mother. Your blood does not coarse through her veins. My blood runs through them now. You are nothing. You are worthless. She is mine now. You can do nothing.

The books on the shelves in the living room began to shake and throw themselves down. An antique vase smashed on its own accord. Pictures on the walls began to fall, the glass protecting the photos shattering. Delana screamed.

Then there was a knock at the door. Delana felt she was rooted in place. She couldn't get herself to answer the door. She was afraid to see who – or what – was on the other side.

"Open the door!" thundered an authoritarian voice.

Delana yelled, "It won't let me!"

The voice on the other side of the door screamed. Delana was certain the neighbors could hear. He yelled, "By the power of the Lord Jesus Christ, I command you, foul spirit, let me into this house of God!"

House of God, Delana thought furiously. *This is a house of evil now. This is a house of sexual deviancy.*

Stop it. Those are not your thoughts.

They are not yours.

This is NOT a house of sexual deviancy!!

The door threw itself open. It was so violent that the door had practically jumped out of the bolts holding it to the frame. A man stood outside, eyes wide in shock. His eyes jumped over to Delana, who was frantically sobbing. He ran over to her. Everything had stopped. Books were ripped open. The vase she had adored was shattered.

Pastor Louis took the woman into his arms and hugged her. Delana didn't want him to let go. "Tell me what's going on," he whispered.

Delana told him what she and Terri had walked in on. She told him about the voice in her head, despite her mind telling her to silence herself. She knew it wasn't her thoughts. She knew they were not hers.

Then a scream pierced the house.

Delana rushed into Amanda's room, Louis barely a foot behind her. Louis took in the scene. It was definitely coming from Terri. She was moaning in pain, trying to get closer to her daughter, but failing in her goal. A child dressed in red was pulling her away, and it was leaving red marks on her hands. On her bare arms.

Amanda stared into Louis's eyes. He had recalled what Terri had told him about her eyes, how they no longer held that loving, innocent light. Instead, he was staring into darkness.

"Welcome to our hell-hole," whispered Delana.

Louis moved his hand into his pocket, holding a cross. Amanda snickered.

"You think that'll do any good?" taunted the little girl. She snickered again.

Louis began to recite a prayer he learned a week ago. He didn't feel confident, but anything would work.

The candles went out, and they were now surrounded in perfect darkness. Louis tried to adjust his sight so he could see, but it wasn't happening. But he felt a change in the air. He could sense something was happening in front of him, but he wasn't able to see shit.

"Welcome to our hell-hole!" thundered a voice that clearly wasn't Delana's.

Something came over Louis as he rushed over to the little girl, who was now floating three feet above the floor. His sight had finally adjusted, but he didn't feel the shock that would've overwhelmed someone who stumbled upon a horrific scene. He took a deep breath and held the cross in front of Amanda.

"Leave this child, Satan! Leave—"

A laugh emitted from Amanda's lips as the cross flew out of his hands. "Your God will not win, Louis Graham Nygaard."

He was hoping that something convenient would occur. He hoped that whatever evil presence would bring her to the bed, and she would be a modern reenactment of a classic horror movie, but that didn't happen. Instead, Amanda's body did a peculiar acrobatic act in the air. But this circus performance befalling everyone's eyes was not amusing.

"Do you have holy water?" Terri asked as she groped around in the darkness for the pastor's cross. "Anything other than this?"

She handed it to him, placing it feebly into his shaking hands. "I don't," he confessed. "Seminary training did not prepare me for this kind of thing!"

Amanda laughed again. "You foolish man," she said in her voice. Her voice changed – her voice was now mixed in with another child's voice. "You come not prepared for a fight, and you will lose. All of you will lose!" She pointed at everyone in the room.

None of them saw the other man sneaking into the room. But Amanda saw something shining. Her head snapped toward the door.

Just as Ian was about to walk into the room, his gun aimed, the door slammed in his face. Amanda laughed.

"He will not win, either!" Amanda said. She motioned her fingers, clenching them together.

"Who are you, foul spirit?" Louis spurted out. "Give me your name!"

Instead of answering, Amanda snickered.

"Tell me your name!"

"I am the little girl, dressed in red. But I am the dead one, watching your every move until the day you die."

"There were two girls, dressed in red," Terri responded. Louis's head snapped over at her as he told her to not speak to the demon.

"Amanda is the other! The one who attempted to protect you from me, but a human spirit is weak in comparison to mine!"

But Amanda never wore that color, Terri thought to herself.

"I never said she was dressed in red clothes," sneered Amanda.

But that makes no sense, Delana thought to herself.

"Her skin is as red as blood, you dumb bitch!" the demon snarled.

"Stop thinking! Do not talk to her!" Louis shouted.

The door opened, but this time it was Ian who opened the door. He took in the room. "What is this?"

"This is the day you die!" thundered the demon.

Something threw Ian across the room. The gun he was holding flew out of his hands in the process. He tried to look up, but he couldn't get his head to move.

Terri expected the pastor to tell the demon to let him go, but he didn't. Instead, he slowly approached her. He lifted the cross up to her, this time holding it tighter than before. Amanda cried out in pain. "Stop what you're doing, fraud!"

But he didn't stop. He could feel a force trying to fight him, but he bested the sensation creeping upon him. He walked behind her, his legs touching her bed.

"You're gonna rape me, aren't you?" taunted the demon.

No reply came out of Louis.

Instead, he forced the cross against her back. Amanda yelped, falling down to the ground. He took advantage of the situation and kept the cross in place, ushering the adults to get her onto the bed. She was groaning, speaking in a language all but one person in the room could understand.

Ian got up from his place on the floor while the pastor kept a hand against Amanda's back, and the women placed her carefully on the bed. Louis kept the cross on her at all times as he readjusted the cross, touching Amanda's neck. In his amazement, he saw red marks appear around the area where the cross was.

"What are you doing to her?" Ian cried out.

"A very unorthodox, impromptu exorcism," Louis replied back.

Ian didn't know how to respond to that. Instead, he just watched in amazement as the pastor began to say something under his breath. Whatever he was doing, it seemed to exacerbate Amanda – or whatever the fuck that thing was.

"Amanda, please," Terri cried, "Please. I know you're with me. I know you're here with us. Fight this, honey. Fight this with everything you've got. Please, honey. Do it for mommy."

Louis looked up at her. "Delana. I need you to speak to Amanda. Not to the demon. I… I think it's working!"

Delana replied back almost the same thing Terri was saying, but she sounded even more empathic than Terri did. She was crying as she spoke with such authority. "Amanda, sweetheart. I love you so much. And I need you to fight this… fight this thing. I know you can. You're a strong little girl. A beautiful child. Please. Listen to your mommies."

Ian had to clutch his hands against his ears as the demon shrilled in a volume that would've made even the strongest glass break. In the process, he stood up and witnessed something remarkable: there was a heavy red cloud leaving the child's lips. Before he fainted from the sound of the demon screaming and screeching, he heard the pastor yell at the cloud.

THERE WAS NO more fear in the house. No anxiety. Nothing negative pounded against the walls of the home anymore. It was beautiful. It was amazing.

Amanda laid in bed, blinking her eyes. A smile creeped over her small face as she looked over and saw the number of stuffed toys she didn't recognize. She let out a small giggle as she saw a box of candies and a lot of cards that told her to get well. She slowly reached her feet down on the ground, moving toward the candies. Terri never let her have anything sweet until the afternoon, most days. But maybe if she allowed herself to have one little chocolate ball, it wouldn't be the end of the world.

She looked at the cards and picked one up. It was from one of her classmates; the small cursive telling her that she was awesome making her laugh out loud. Another card – one from the school counselor – told her that she was loved.

She didn't hear her mom come into the room and watch her daughter. She smiled as Amanda opened the little box of chocolates and take one, unwrapping it and placing it gently on her tongue. "Is it okay if I have one?" asked Delana.

Amanda jumped back. "Umm," she started.

"We won't tell Mom, okay?" said Delana as she walked over to Amanda.

Amanda took another one out of the box, handing it to Delana. She opened it and popped it in her mouth. "Ooh, that one might be my favorite. Caramel."

Amanda grinned, revealing chocolate-stained teeth.

Delana returned the teeth-stained smile to her daughter.

"You feeling good enough to help me make breakfast?" asked Delana. "Whatever you want."

"Scrambled eggs and bacon? With toast and chocolate?"

Delana laughed. "That sounds awesome! Let's go get your mom."

They left the room, walking into the kitchen. Ian and Louis were there, talking with Terri in the living room. She looked up at them, making the international sign for "close the kitchen door" to Delana. She nodded in understanding and closed the door. She was curious to know what they were talking about but knew better than to eavesdrop.

Terri asked Pastor Louis, "Will she remember anything?"

"I don't think she will. What she went through is enough to traumatize even the most resilient man that walks the earth," Louis replied. "Trauma like that experienced by a child like yours? She won't remember."

Ian coughed. "That was traumatizing, that's for damn sure."

Terri looked at the detective. "What are you going to do?"

Ian didn't reply right away. He looked at the kitchen door, then looked back at the package next to him. "I want to speak to Amanda, alone, if that's all right."

"I don't know if that's such a good idea," Terri said as she eyed the package. "And what's in that box?"

Ian patted the package. "I guess it's all right if you're here for this."

Ian's lack of response wasn't one to worry about. She knew he wouldn't harm her daughter. He loved her as though he were her father. She had attempted to phone Jeff earlier but was interrupted by the unexpected visit by both Louis and Ian. She wanted to tell him, and both men thought it was a good idea, as long as she only provided vague answers for the time being. She finally got ahold of her ex-husband about ten minutes later, but he had to go right away to do something for the restaurant.

Terri got up from her comfortable chair and entered the kitchen. "Amanda?"

Amanda turned toward her mom and smiled. "I love you, mommy."

Terri grinned as though she could never frown again. "The nice cop has something for you. Can I steal your chef-in-training away for a second?"

Delana nodded her head, and Terri took her daughter by her hand. Amanda's grip was firm. But it was a welcoming touch to her. It was as though she was gripping her hand as a way of saying, thank you. The touch Terri was feeling against her hand was a loving touch, a protective touch.

"Hey, kiddo," Ian said as he lifted the box from the couch. "Got something for you."

Amanda's eyes glowed in excitement. "Ooh, what is it?" she said as she ran into Ian's arms. He laughed as he embraced her.

"Open it," he mouthed to her.

She practically tore the box, revealing a beautiful stuffed dog. Terri glared at Ian, mouthing, "What the fuck is wrong with you?"

But he pretended as though he didn't hear her. "I got it from the store," he explained. "A chain store."

Terri shook her head in amusement. She looked up at him and smiled. "I don't think I'll be selling any more toys in the antique shop, for the time being."

"Might be a good idea," Louis replied, grinning. "If you change your mind in the future, lemme know."

"What are they talking about, Mommy?" Amanda asked, petting the dog's head.

"Nothing to worry about," Terri responded, still smiling. "Nothing to worry about at all."

IT HAD BEEN a long, yet wonderful day. Delana took

all of them out for a celebratory dinner. Amanda asked what they were celebrating, and she said that they were celebrating Amanda. Celebrating her health. Amanda giggled as she took a bite of her pasta. Delana looked over at Terri. She was also smiling, watching her daughter eat her pasta voraciously. The "illness" which had ailed her daughter really took a toll on her daughter, but after a short conversation with her, she concluded that Amanda remembered literally nothing about the past couple weeks.

Jeff walked over to the table and was surprised by a genuine, loving hug by all the women sitting at the table. He had taken care of everything. In fact, Delana and Jeff worked together to celebrate the event. Terri was happy to see both of them working together and becoming friends.

When they got home, Delana took Amanda into the bathroom to get ready for bed. Terri yawned, walking into her room to prepare to go to bed.

Sitting on the bed was Violet Red.

Terri shuddered.

Not again.

Please, not again.

Carefully, Terri slipped on her gloves that were sitting in her dresser drawer and touched the toy around its body. She looked at Violet Red, wondering just how a beautiful object, a toy meant for children, could be a… oh what was the word… a conduit for something evil.

But she wasn't unprepared for this.

When Louis dropped by, he handed her a box, in case anything were to happen again. It was blessed by a holy man who was known in the church to be a powerhouse. She just didn't expect…

She didn't think she would have to do what she would have to do.

She opened the box and placed the toy in it, silently whispering a prayer to keep this evil object away from her daughter. Terri clutched the box with the gloves, just to be safe, and opened the ceiling door, leading to the attic. Terri placed the box in the far corner of the room, still praying that this toy would never feel the touch of Amanda's hands, let alone another child's, ever again. A grin of triumph made itself known to her as she walked out of the attic, knowing her home was now demon-free, knowing that her daughter was now alive and well, not plagued by anything not of this world. She was happier than Terri could ever remember.

But no matter how happy and how healthy Amanda was, there were still scars from the exorcism that Louis didn't think would ever disappear. She concocted the perfect story to ensure her daughter's safety, to ensure that Amanda would never remember the horror she went through. Terri hoped it would be good enough to satiate any curiosity Amanda would have, later in life. She asked Louis if this lie was okay in the eyes of the God he worshipped. He looked at her, smiled, and said, "What lie?"

Terri looked around her house as she left the darkness of the attic. This house, this home, was now a beacon of light – a warm light of love and health. But inside that box, tucked away in the attic? It was still a beacon of darkness, of illness, *of obsession*, wanting to let itself out.

Supposedly...
Allegedly...

THE END

THE STORY OF VIOLET RED
CONTINUES WITH…

VIOLET RED #2
THEN COMES POSSESSION

ACKNOWLEDGEMENTS

This story came about one afternoon while at work. One of my coworkers brought in a decorative toy for her cubicle. If you squeezed its body, it would tell the user that they were loved. It had this creepy voice, and I couldn't help but cringe when she pressed on the toy.

I think it was about an hour later when I heard it go off. I wasn't the only one surprised – my coworker was just as taken aback as I was. She persisted in telling us she didn't touch it. She didn't touch it at all! It was probably an older plaything; its batteries were not as strong as they once were. But hearing that little stuffed, inanimate object emit that creepy voice, telling me that it loved me, was enough to warrant inspiration.

Then there was that nagging rhyme that wouldn't leave my mind: "Two little girls dressed in red/One girl alive, the other one dead/Don't close your eyes, don't rest your head/She is watching – the dead girl in red."

But this inspiration goes even further back. My best friend at the time owned a Furby when it was popular to have one. I hated those things and Adam knew damn well how much I hated it. I recall telling him to take the batteries out and leave it in the closet. As we were watching something on the tv in his room, we heard the Furby go off. We looked at each other – *we fucking removed the batteries!*

Almost reminds you of Chucky, doesn't it?

Violet Red is inspired by those two moments of toys acting peculiar. Objects like the Furby and the stuffed animal thing on my coworker's desk are intentionally created for children. Little, innocent children. But what if that toy you got at a second-hand store wasn't meant for an innocent child? In the introduction to J. W. Ocker's book, *Cursed Objects*, the author says that anything can be cursed, and the thing that really sucks about cursed objects is that you won't know *until it's too late*.

Such is the case with Violet Red. Terri and Amanda do not realize that this seemingly innocent stuffed dog is a conduit until it's too late. According to demonologist Ed Warren, objects like Annabelle and Violet Red are conduits for inhuman spirits. You must allow them into your life for the entity to make itself known. Violet Red is the same as Annabelle, yet different in certain ways. For Amanda, her obsession over the stuffed dog brought the entity into her life. She allowed the obsession to take over her.

Since my coworker was the one who really inspired this tale of terror, I want to thank her for giving me the idea. Her interest and passion for antique stores are the reason why Terri owns TerriRific Antiques. My coworker's knowledge of antiques and passion for good finds was very helpful in the composition of this story.

For gay and lesbian people who lived in the 90s, reading and listening to stories of people who lived in that time was also very helpful. While the 1990s brings about nostalgia for me with shows and toys I enjoyed, it cannot be denied that homophobia was a part of that decade. Doctors, police officers, among other professionals (and still do, to this day), have antiquated and harmful perspectives on LGBT+ people. Not only is this story a horror story in terms of the supernatural, but it also exposes the dark reality of what life would have been like for two women who lived together during that time period, fighting a broken system just so they can still raise a child.

If there's anything that should be taken from this novel, it's this: sometimes the best thing you need to do in order to live your life to the maximum is to lock and bolt anything that hinders your happiness and health. Nothing is worth the pain and sorrow of hiding who you truly are.

ALSO AVAILABLE ON AMAZON

Before Derek L. Davis wrote Their Eyes Were Black and his debut horror novel, Evil Has A Target, he dabbled in writing short stories self-published on the Lulu platform. Now, for the very first time in years, Derek has brought back those stories and has revived them. Everything you will be reading in this collection are all of the short stories Derek has composed, left untouched and forgotten on the Lulu site, going back to the early 2000s. Even though these stories are what the author considers to be juvenile, they show something of who the writer used to be. They show a young writer who would eventually grow up to be a better one. These stories are a historical, dynamic record of creative growth, going back to the year 2000 and up to 2022, with five new stories, including a short story one never before seen by others until now.

SOCIAL MEDIA

FACEBOOK = @derekldavis

TWITTER = @DerekWithBooks

INSTAGRAM = @derekwithabook

www.ingramcontent.com/pod-product-compliance
Lightning Source LLC
La Vergne TN
LVHW012051160826
845678LV00014B/2786

9798841674719